Better Think Twice . . .

Slocum squeezed off a shot.

A black hole appeared in the center of Fisk's forehead and he dropped the shotgun, falling forward and crashing into Scudder. This threw the sheriff off balance as he clawed for his pistol.

Slocum scrambled to his feet, stepped toward Scudder.

"You draw that hogleg, Scudder," Slocum said, "and I'll put a bullet where your grub goes."

Scudder froze, his right hand turned into a rigid claw inches from his pistol.

"You bastard," Scudder snarled. "I know who you are. You're a wanted man, John Slocum . . ."

JAKE LOGAN

SLOCUM
AND THE
CANYON COURTESANS

J

JOVE BOOKS, NEW YORK

THE BERKLEY PUBLISHING GROUP
Published by the Penguin Group
Penguin Group (USA) Inc.
375 Hudson Street, New York, New York 10014, USA

Penguin Group (Canada), 90 Eglinton Avenue East, Suite 700, Toronto, Ontario M4P 2Y3, Canada
(a division of Pearson Penguin Canada Inc.) • Penguin Books Ltd., 80 Strand, London WC2R 0RL,
England • Penguin Group Ireland, 25 St. Stephen's Green, Dublin 2, Ireland (a division of Penguin
Books Ltd.) • Penguin Group (Australia), 250 Camberwell Road, Camberwell, Victoria 3124, Australia
(a division of Pearson Australia Group Pty. Ltd.) • Penguin Books India Pvt. Ltd., 11 Community
Centre, Panchsheel Park, New Delhi—110 017, India • Penguin Group (NZ), 67 Apollo Drive,
Rosedale, Auckland 0632, New Zealand (a division of Pearson New Zealand Ltd.) • Penguin Books
(South Africa) (Pty.) Ltd., 24 Sturdee Avenue, Rosebank, Johannesburg 2196, South Africa

Penguin Books Ltd., Registered Offices: 80 Strand, London WC2R 0RL, England

SLOCUM AND THE CANYON COURTESANS

A Jove Book / published by arrangement with the author

PUBLISHING HISTORY
Jove edition / June 2012

Copyright © 2012 by Penguin Group (USA) Inc.
Cover illustration by Sergio Giovine.

ISBN: 978-0-515-15094-0

JOVE®
Jove Books are published by The Berkley Publishing Group,
a division of Penguin Group (USA) Inc.,
375 Hudson Street, New York, New York 10014.
JOVE® is a registered trademark of Penguin Group (USA) Inc.
The "J" design is a trademark of Penguin Group (USA) Inc.

PRINTED IN THE UNITED STATES OF AMERICA

10 9 8 7 6 5 4 3 2 1

ALWAYS LEARNING   **PEARSON**

1

The wind scoured his face, blistered his cracked lips, stung his earlobes like angry wasps. His black shirt and trousers were flocked with the powdery granules of red dust. His nostrils and lips were limned with the flotsam blown by the vicious West Texas wind, and the sky was filled with a rosy haze as if trying to smother all life with its monstrous choking cloud.

Slocum bent over his horse's neck as if to find shelter, but it was like riding into a tunnel of crimson fumes that strangled horse and rider. The brim of his hat fluttered like a banging shutter, the thong dug into his dust-corded neck as if trying to take flight and sail like a kite across Palo Duro Canyon, that desolate wasteland a hundred yards away from a trail that was all but obliterated by the slashing lash of the wind.

It was then that Slocum heard a faint cry from somewhere in the bowels of the rugged canyon. Was it just a shriek of wind caroming off a stunted pine or whistling through a juniper standing on tiptoe in a pile of rocks? He did not know, but it was a disturbing sound and his instincts demanded that he investigate the source. Mingled with those instincts were a hunch and a curiosity that wiped out any sensible objections. He looked back at the four horses he was leading. He did not want to take them down into the forbidding canyon, so he looked for a place to ground-tie them while he investigated.

He had ridden down from Amarillo the day before, and had since covered some thirty miles as he headed toward Charlie Goodnight's ranch.

He found a thick clump of sagebrush and dismounted, wrapping the rope around the base of the large bush, and tying a large loose knot to hold the rope in place, securing the four horses. He climbed back on his black horse, Ferro, and rode toward the rim of the canyon.

Again he heard the soft scream, and he knew it was not a trick of the wind.

It was a woman's cry that he heard and it was laden with notes of helplessness and terror, a pathetic cry for help. He loosened the '73 Winchester in its scabbard and lifted the butt of his Colt .45 from its holster and then eased it back into the leather, ready to draw at an instant's notice.

He clapped his stovepipe boots into Ferro's flanks and began to descend into the canyon. The ground rose up under the horse's hooves, rugged and rocky, with sandy patches that gave way under the iron shoes so that they slid off trail a time or two until the horse regained its footing. Wary, Slocum's green eyes narrowed and his head turned in a semicircle to take in every rock, cactus, clump of sage, yucca, and creosote bush. He looked for movement, for anything out of place.

He reined up Ferro when he saw the wheel of a wagon suspended in midair. It was not spinning, but frozen there like some cockeyed remnant slanted at an acute angle that was far from normal. He nudged Ferro forward over a little rise and saw the wagon tilted over on its side, the canvas strangely taut and lifeless in the windless air of a deep arroyo.

The ground was strewn with clothing as if a laundry basket had been emptied. He saw women's bloomers, stockings, underpants, brassieres, lace skirts, and a green bustle, glistening like a large bug in the sunlight. The wagon tongue lay stretched out, its traces cut, and in the wagon seat, a man's legs dangled over the side.

As he rode down, he saw a couple of tattered silk purses, empty hatboxes, and three hats that appeared to have been ground into the dirt by horses. The wagon tongue pointed to a small water hole ringed with mud scarred with unshod pony hooves. The fresh tracks were already drying in the sun but were distinct enough to tell a small story to a man who was used to reading sign.

He heard a low moan coming from the other side of the overturned wagon. He steered Ferro toward the sound, his right hand gripping the butt of his pistol, which was halfway out of its holster.

"Man, you got to help me," croaked a voice from beneath the wagon.

Slocum looked down and saw an outstretched hand, the arm sleeved in chambray soaked with blood.

"You crawl out from under there and show me both hands," Slocum said.

"Jesus. I'm hurt real bad."

"Crawl out and I'll take a look at you."

"Leastways you talk like a white man."

There was a scuffling sound and another hand appeared, clawing at the ground. The man pulled himself out in a slow crawl, and Slocum saw that he was young and hatless, with streaks of blood on the shoulders and back of his shirt. The man looked up beseechingly with his terror-filled eyes, eyes that bulged from their sockets and were plainly bloodshot. Slocum saw that the man was unarmed, wore no gun belt. He dismounted and spoke a low word to Ferro.

He walked over and pulled the man out. The man winced with pain and Slocum saw that a round patch had been cut in the front of his skull, the hair yanked off, leaving a patch of white skull partially covered with the curly hair that grew around it.

"Can you stand up?" Slocum asked.

"N-N-No," the man stammered. "I—I'm gutshot."

Slocum turned the man over and saw the purple-gray gleam of intestines. Blood oozed from the wound in his abdomen. Bluebottle flies swarmed around the putrid coils of smashed intestines.

"What's your name?" Slocum asked.

"Why do you want to know?" The man grimaced in pain, but Slocum knew that he had been in shock. Probably hadn't felt much pain when he got shot and scalped. But now his nerve ends were jumping like ants in a brushfire.

"I'll probably say a few words over you before I bury you," Slocum said.

"Huh?"

"Your name, son."

"I—it's Jeremy. Jeremy Slater. Am I gonna die?"

"Sure as I'm standing here, Jeremy. You've lost about two quarts of blood and I'm all out of needle and thread."

"Jesus," Slater said.

"You might want to say a prayer right about now," Slocum said. "What happened here anyway?"

"Bunch of Injuns come swarmin' down on us as we was makin' for the water hole. I don't know, 'Paches or Kiowas, a-screamin' and shootin'. They kilt Ruddy Dover, right off. He was the driver. I was just along to help with the horses. Jesus, I'm getting dizzy."

"You're leaking blood like a water spigot," Slocum said.

Slater's eyes seemed to lose focus as they filled with tears.

"Can't you do somethin'?" Slater asked.

Slocum shook his head. "You're leaking blood like a sieve, Jeremy. There's no way to cauterize a wound like that."

"Jesus," Slater said again.

"I heard a scream," Slocum said. "A woman's scream. Know who it was? Or where she was?"

"I—I think that was Melissa. Melissa Warren. Them Injuns took the other gals, and the horses. Yippin' and hollerin' like all get-out."

"How did Melissa escape being captured?"

Slater started to shake his head, but winced in pain. He looked up at the sky as if to avoid seeing what had happened to his abdomen.

"Wh-When the wagon went over, the other gals all screamed and huddled up. Melissa, she—she fell out and crawled up into them rocks yonder before the Injuns come down and grabbed all the gals and jerked them outen the wagon."

Slocum looked up at the other side of the canyon. There were dark holes in the jumble of rocks and vegetation, small openings that could have been caves, hiding places for coyotes, pumas, or skunks. There was no sign of life at any of the holes or the surrounding terrain.

He returned his gaze to Slater, whose jaw tightened so that he wore a pained grimace on his face.

Slater looked up at the tall man wearing a black hat with a silver band, a black shirt, black trousers, and black boots. The .45 Colt on his hip was black, too, and the cartridges in his gun belt glistened golden in the sun.

"You a gunslinger?" Slater asked. "You look mean as hell."

"An outlaw, you mean," Slocum said.

"Well, yeah, I guess so."

"I carry a gun for protection," Slocum said.

"You—You look like you could use it, all right."

Slocum said nothing. Slater was bleeding to death and he probably would not last much longer. His breathing had become shallower, and his face was paling beneath the sweat. He noticed a slight tremor in the dying man's hands.

His fingers were beginning to twitch and his hands shook. He had seen men die before. A lot of times the pain went away just before they breathed their last breath, and they seemed to settle into a kind of final peace. Slater appeared to be slipping out of pain and into some deeper state that was more like a numbness throughout his body, a final breakdown of nerves that signaled death just a few breaths away.

Just then, Slocum heard a low moan from somewhere up on the hillside, then a soft sob and a pathetic and pitiful cry for help.

He looked up, but could not tell where the sounds had come from because the cave entrances were black as pitch and there was no movement in any of them.

"Sounds like Melissa," Slater gruffed, his voice as scratchy as if it had been rubbed with sandpaper. Blood bubbled up in his throat and he choked, spat a spray of thin red fluid from his mouth. His body shuddered and his eyes rolled back in their sockets, showing the whites. Blood gurgled in his throat as he tried to clear it, and when he opened his mouth to speak or to cry out some last utterance, there was an ominous rattle that seemed to come from deep in his sunken chest.

Ferro pawed the ground with his right hoof and whickered softly.

Slater's body quivered and he closed his eyes.

His last breath was a weary sigh as his eyes opened one last time and stared lifeless into eternity.

2

Slocum heard a disturbance at the same time as he looked up and saw a young woman begin to emerge from one of the caves.

He drew his pistol and yelled: "Stay there."

The woman ducked back into the cave. Slocum turned and cocked his pistol. He began to run up the hill he had recently climbed down.

The horses he had tied up screamed in terror, their high-pitched whinnies sending a rippling chill up his spine. As he topped the ridge, he saw three painted warriors, driving the horses away from where they had been tethered. One of the men turned and fired a rifle at Slocum. His face was smeared with streaks of white, red, and yellow war paint.

The bullet from the Spencer carbine sizzled over Slocum's head. He ducked and heard the bullet whine off a rock on the opposite slope of the canyon. The horses and the Indians disappeared over a rise as Slocum eased the hammer down on his pistol. The Indians were too far way and traveling far too fast for him to catch up to them. Besides, he figured there were others waiting in some wash or gully to ambush anyone who followed the horse thieves.

He looked down at the ground and saw the tracks left behind. Three unshod horses and four wearing iron shoes. They would be easy to track, he thought, since the ground was dry and the sand loose. He sensed that there had been no rain in that part of Texas for quite a spell.

Slocum holstered his pistol and walked back down to where Ferro stood hipshot. He walked on a slant down into the canyon to lessen the pull of gravity on his large frame. The horse whickered softly and Slocum looked up at the cave as he drew up alongside his horse.

"You can come out now, missy," he called.

He saw a hand emerge from the hole, then another, and a few minutes later, the young woman crawled on her knees onto a small ledge. She stared down at him, and he could see that she was trembling.

She looked all around, blinking her eyes as if adjusting them to the strong sunlight.

"Can you get down by yourself?" he asked.

"Are you Mr. Bascomb?" she asked. There was a look of bewilderment in her eyes.

"No," he said, "I'm John Slocum."

"Did Mr. Bascomb send you?"

"No, ma'am. I don't know Bascomb. I was just passing by and heard you scream."

"Is Jerry—is he . . ."

"He's dead, ma'am."

"Oh no," she exclaimed.

"Yes'm, I'm afraid so."

The woman stood up. Slocum watched as she swayed for a minute, then regained her composure and began to pick her way down the slope.

"Miss Warren?" he said as she stumbled toward him. She glanced at the body of Jeremy Slater, then turned quickly away, where her gaze rested on Slocum's face.

"I'm Melissa Warren," she said. "Who are you?"

"I'm John Slocum. Can you tell me anything about what happened here and where you and the three other women were headed?"

She looked around at all the clothing, carpetbags, purses, hats, and she shivered.

"We were going to a place called Quitaque," she said. "Four of us from Duluth."

"Minnesota?"

"Yes," she said. "The coldest place on earth. Or at least in the United States."

"What was in Quitaque?"

"Husbands," she said meekly, and hung her head as if she were ashamed.

"You gals were mail-order brides?"

"I—I guess that's what we were, or thought we were. Then this happened."

"I've got some burying to do," he said. "You might want to change clothes or find your things. We'll ride double, so you can't pack much."

"Where are you taking me?" she asked.

"I lost four good horses to those Kiowa and you lost three friends. I'm going after those redskins."

"There were at least six of them," she said. "What can you do against so many?"

He tapped the butt of his Colt.

"They have guns, too, mister."

"Single-shot carbines."

"You live by the gun, Mr. Slocum?"

"I keep mine handy. It's a tool, like any other."

"A tool?"

"Like a hammer. Only mine comes with its own nails."

She brushed dirt and sand from her blouse and tried to smooth her skirt.

"I won't change," she said, "but I'd like to carry some clothes in a carpetbag if you don't mind."

"We can tie the bag in back of my saddle," he said.

She began to gather a few items of clothing and place them in a small carpetbag. Slocum found a shovel lashed to the side of the overturned wagon and dug two shallow graves. He went through the pockets of the dead men, but found only a few silver dollars and a double eagle, which he pocketed. Neither man wore a sidearm, and if there had been a scattergun or rifle in the wagon, the Kiowa had taken it. The man in the wagon seat appeared to be in his late forties or early fifties. He was balding and had salt-and-pepper sideburns. Slocum put both men in the ground, covered them with dirt, and then placed rocks atop the mounds.

He stood there at the head of the two graves and took off his hat.

"Lord," he intoned, "I ask that you take these two souls and put them in your care. Amen."

"Are you a religious man, Mr. Slocum?" Melissa asked as Slocum placed his hat back on his head.

"Not particularly. But they might have been."

"But you said a prayer for them."

"Couldn't hurt," he said.

She gave him a baleful glance and picked up her carpetbag. She handed it to him and he tied it in back of his saddle, behind the bedroll already there.

"I'll mount up first, then you step into the stirrup and I'll pull you up. You ride behind me. You can straddle on that carpetbag."

She nodded and watched him pick up his reins and climb into the saddle.

"This is a tall horse," she said.

"Yes'm. His name's Ferro."

"Ferro? That's an odd name."

"It means 'iron' in Spanish. Sometimes I think he's made of it. He's a right strong horse."

He pulled her up and she slid in behind the cantle, sat on

the carpetbag, which mashed down and made for a comfortable seat. Her arms hung at her sides.

"You might want to hold on to my gun belt or put your arms around my waist," he said. "Otherwise, you might fall off and get trampled."

"I've never ridden a horse before," she said.

"A good time to learn," he said.

She put her arms around his waist. Slocum ticked Ferro's flanks with his blunt spurs and they climbed out of the canyon, rode back to the place where he had left the four horses the Kiowa had stolen. He rode south, following the tracks.

Melissa tightened her grip around his waist as Slocum put the horse into a trot.

"There's something I forgot to tell you, Mr. Slocum," she said.

"You can call me John, miss."

"Well, then, you can call me Mel, or Melissa."

"Which do you prefer?" he said, tilting his head so that she could hear him. The tracks were plain on the dry ground—four shod horses, three unshod ponies. Smaller tracks for the ponies and not as distinct as those made by the iron shoes.

"Melissa, I guess. That's what my ma called me. My pa and my brothers called me Mel, and some of the people I've met want to shorten my name. But Mel is a man's name, I reckon."

"Yeah," he said. "I'd take it for a man's name. Melissa, it is. Now, what is it you wanted to tell me?"

"I thought it odd, but I was so scared, I wasn't thinking straight. I thought the Injuns were going to kill us all after they shot those two men off the wagon seat. But one of the men who rode down on us wasn't an Injun."

"What do you mean?"

Slocum slowed the horse and turned his head to glimpse part of Melissa's face.

"I mean that there was a white man with those Injuns. White as you or me. He didn't have paint on his face, and he wore a big old hat with a funny band around it. Looked like snakeskin."

Slocum reined up and turned in the saddle to look directly at Melissa.

"Did you ever see the man before?" he asked. "Did you hear his name?"

"I never saw him before," she said. "But one of the Injuns he spoke to called him Scud. At least it sounded like 'Scud' to me."

"Scud? Funny name," he said.

"That's what I thought. At first I thought the Injun was saying 'Spud,' but another one said his name and I'm pretty sure it was 'Scud.'"

"That's good to know," he said, and turned back to look down at the tracks. He rode on, thinking about what she had told him.

Strange, he thought. What was a white man doing with a bunch of renegade Indians? And what did he want with three or four single women?

Nothing good, he surmised.

The tracks showed him that the horses were no longer running. The Kiowa had slowed them to a walk a mile or two from where the horses had been rustled. The sun beat down on him, and he felt a wetness under his shirt where Melissa's hands were holding on to him.

The tracks headed south, parallel to Palo Duro Canyon.

They headed south to God knew where.

3

Melissa nestled her head against Slocum's back. She looked at the bleak landscape passing by and licked her dry lips. She was thirsty and tired. And, she thought, she was entirely at the mercy of this tall man whom she did not know at all.

"Where are we going?" she asked. "To Quitaque?"

"Those Kiowa stole four horses I was taking to the Good-night ranch," he said. "I aim to get them back."

"Horses? We're following horses?"

"And three Kiowa braves who stole them," he said.

"What about my friends who were kidnapped? Aren't they a lot more important than horses?"

"Your friends are heading the same way as my horses," he said. "If you look down at the ground, you'll see a lot more tracks than when we started."

Melissa looked down at the ground. It was a maze of horse tracks. Her eyes blurred as she tried to separate them. There were dozens of hoof marks in the dry earth, and they were all heading in the same direction. Some tracks were deeper than others, some more distinct.

"How can you make any sense out of such a jumble of horse tracks?" she asked.

"It takes some practice," he said. "And a lot of experience."

"I wouldn't know one track from another," she said.

"Well, here and now, all these tracks are important, Melissa. I figure two of the women are riding on the two horses that pulled that wagon. Actually, I think one of those horses is packing double. Three Kiowa are pulling my horses behind theirs."

"You can tell all that just from those tracks? I can't see much difference between one horse or another."

"The Kiowa are riding unshod ponies. The white man you said was named Scud is riding a shod horse. The two horses that pulled the wagon are wearing new iron shoes. The depth of the hoof marks tells me that one of those is carrying more weight than the other. The horses are all packed close together, with the two horses carrying the women in a box surrounded by Kiowa. The man called Scud is in the lead."

"You make it sound like reading a book," she said.

"Tracks can tell a pretty clear story," he said. "You just have to know how to read them."

"I'm amazed."

"When I was a boy back in Calhoun County in Georgia, my pa made me look at all kinds of animal tracks. Once, he set me on a patch of ground, made me lie down and watch the ants and bugs for half a day. He took me on walks through the woods and told me how to tell the age of a deer track by the amount of moisture in it and whether the earth at the top was starting to crumble. He did that with quail, turkey, squirrels, raccoons, and possums."

"Did you enjoy doing all that?" she asked, her voice jiggling as they rode over a patch of rough ground.

"Yes. I learned a lot and maybe I thought I was reading the minds of the game animals. I could look at a quail wallow and see where they dusted their bodies and wings and then follow their tracks and find a covey to flush and shoot. Meat for the table."

"It sounds almost like you were one of the animals."

Slocum laughed.

"Sometimes, I probably was. All animals hunt for food. They might hunt berries or sweet grass, but some of them hunt meat. Everything wild hunts something else."

"Is that how you feel now, John?"

He let out a breath, a deep sigh.

"I'm hunting, all right," he said.

"I hope you don't mind my asking all these questions," she said.

"I don't mind, but best you keep quiet from now on. Those Kiowa can be mighty sneaky and I have to keep my wits about me."

"Seems to me you have a tight grip on your wits, John," she said.

"Well, the Kiowa have a habit of watching their back trail, and one or two of them could be lying behind a bush or a rock ready to shoot me out of the saddle."

"I'll keep quiet," she said.

She scooted closer and pressed against him, holding on with both arms wrapped tightly around his chest. He could feel the soft pressure of her breasts mashed against his back. She was a beautiful young woman with sleek black hair, a perky uptilted nose, and bright blue eyes. She was a few inches over five feet, and, even with that long dress on, he could tell that she had slim legs and pretty ankles. Although she smelled of jasmine perfume, there was the earthy allure of her sweat beneath the fragrance.

They rode on through the blistering hot afternoon. Slocum scanned both sides of the trail and stopped when he saw a change in the tracks. Two of the Indian ponies had left the trail and ridden off toward the canyon. That was ominous enough because they could wait in ambush anywhere along the snaking fissure in the earth and pick him off like a turtle on a log.

He said nothing to Melissa, and continued to follow the main body of horse tracks. To his surprise, after another three miles or so, the tracks also began edging toward Palo Duro Canyon as the sun dipped to a few degrees above the horizon in the west. He turned Ferro to follow the tracks, but his gut clenched as he realized how dangerous it would be to follow the Kiowa and the white man through the canyon.

Slocum did not ride down into the canyon but stayed atop the rim. He could see the tracks on the canyon floor and then they just vanished. He backtracked without speaking to Melissa, and saw where someone had cut branches from a small bush and then begun brushing out the tracks behind the other horses.

The sun hovered over the horizon, a blazing disk of fire that painted the dust and seemed to shimmer like a god's eye over an empty land where nothing moved and their breathing was the only sound.

"There's something wrong, isn't there?" Melissa said, her voice barely above a whisper.

"I don't know. A couple of those braves are brushing out the tracks. They must know that I'm following them."

"What do we do now?" she asked, and there was a faint tremor in her voice.

"We're not going down into that canyon, that's for sure," he said.

"So, we might not be able to follow them."

"When that sun goes down," he said, "these long shadows will disappear and it will be dark as a coal pit until moon-rise. I don't know if they'll ride in the dark or pitch camp down in that canyon. But we'd better scout out a place to spend the night."

She looked around and saw nothing but emptiness. A soft breeze sprang up just then and the air was warm against her face.

"Where?" she asked.

"We have maybe fifteen minutes to a half hour to find a safe place to camp for the night."

"In the canyon, then? It's the only place that will offer us any protection from the wind."

"You know about the wind here in West Texas, then," he said.

"I sure do. The first day out I thought the wagon was going to blow away. I asked Ruddy Dover, the driver, about it. I said, 'Is it always this windy out here?' And he said, 'No, ma'am, sometimes the wind blows real hard.'"

Slocum chuckled.

"He was right. The wind out here can blow a whole town away."

As if to underline his words, the wind began to pick up and their faces stung with blown sand. They ducked and rode on. The dust filled the air with a rosy hue and it was difficult to see.

Just as the sun fell beneath the horizon with only its angry red rim showing in a cloudless sky, Slocum spotted something ahead of them. He rode toward it as the rim of the sun vanished over the horizon.

There, in the middle of that desolate landscape, was a broken-down adobe. Its roof had caved in and the bricks were weatherworn and crumbling, but it still had three walls and some rafters heaped inside.

"What is that?" Melissa asked as they rode up and Slocum circled the abandoned hut.

"An old adobe house gone to ruin," he said.

She shuddered.

"It's probably full of rats and snakes," she said.

"Well, they'll likely run off once we tromp around in there."

"We're going to stay here tonight?"

"It's like a gift from on high," he said with a taunting smile on his face.

"I'll sleep outside, under the stars," she said.

"Suit yourself, Melissa," he replied and smiled again.

He ground-tied Ferro while Melissa wandered off to answer nature's call. He saw signs that told him travelers had camped there before. There were empty tins that once contained coffee, peaches, and other foods, the metal completely rusted, the labels long since eaten or washed away by rain. The rafters made a kind of tent, though, and he scraped his soles across hard-packed dirt where bedrolls had hardened the ground. He carried two canteens, his bedroll, and Melissa's carpetbag inside. He set the bag and canteens in a corner and laid out his blanket. He went back outside, unsaddled Ferro after slipping his Winchester out of its scabbard, and carried his saddle and gun inside.

The wind blew hard and hot, sending waves of sand across the darkening landscape when Melissa returned, her face slightly flushed from the stinging sand. She squinted her eyes and looked at the bedroll all laid out and glanced at her carpetbag in the corner.

"You're welcome to share my makeshift bunk for the night, Melissa," he said, his tone congenial and without any trace of the lust he was beginning to feel.

"No, thank you," she said. "It's hardly big enough for you. And I'm scared of snakes and rats."

She picked up her carpetbag and started to walk outside.

"It can get mighty cold out here at night," he said. "And snakes sniff out warm bodies when it gets like that. I don't see any rat droppings in here. Nothing for them to eat. Might be a termite or two."

"I'm sleeping outside," she said.

Slocum pulled a cheroot from his pocket, lit it with a wooden match he struck on the sole of his boot. He stared out at the sky as the blue faded and the sun glowed in a gray and purple haze far to the west. He listened as he turned his head to pick up any alien sound.

He would not sleep that night, but hold to the adobe shadows with his rifle.

There were Kiowa braves out there, with war paint on their faces.

And he did not know where any of them were.

4

As the darkness deepened, the sky around the adobe was streaked by bullbats, their quarter-sized wing emblems flashing as they darted and twisted in their pursuit of flying insects.

"There must be a creek or a spring somewhere around here," Slocum mused.

"Why do you say that?" she asked.

"Two things. Mosquitoes need standing water to breed and hatch, and whoever built this adobe had to have water."

"It all looks pretty dry to me," she said.

"I've seen signs of flash floods, so either there's a water hole around here, or a creek. I'll look for it in the morning."

"I just want to find those girls I was riding with and get to my destination," she said.

"You might as well be comfortable and lie down on my bedroll. I'm going to stand guard all night."

"Stand guard? Why?"

"The Kiowa," he said.

"You think they know where we are?"

"I'd be surprised if they didn't."

"I don't want to sleep inside that old adobe," she said.

"At least take my blanket, Melissa."

She went inside and picked up his blanket. The makeshift bed looked inviting, but there were too many dark corners in the ruins of the room, and the thought of sleeping inside made her skin crawl with goose bumps.

She walked outside and lay down. She put her head on her carpetbag and pulled the blanket up around her, waist high.

"Sleep tight," Slocum said, and walked to the other side of the adobe, where Ferro was tethered. He patted the horse's withers and then leaned against one of the standing walls of the adobe hut.

The bullbats disappeared as suddenly as they had come. He heard the throaty call of an owl, and an hour or two later, coyotes sounded in the distance, their yodeling voices rising and falling like fountains of the crystalline notes of flutes. His eyelids grew heavy and he walked a circle around the adobe, then another, widening his course through a desolate and lonely world of starlight and a moonglow that gilded all the plants with the dull silver of pewter. It was on one of his circlings that he came upon what appeared to be a small water hole and a well with a rusted pump on it next to a wooden trough that was full of stagnant water. He rubbed the sides and saw that the gaps between the boards had been sealed with thick tar. He worked the pump. It squeaked and groaned, but after pumping it a few times, water spurted out and splashed into the tank.

It was then that Slocum heard a furtive sound. It might have been the snort of a horse, or the cough of a puma, perhaps the rustle of wind in the fallen rafters of the adobe.

He stiffened to a still position and slowly turned his head, straining his ears to pick up the slightest sound.

Then there was another sound, and this time it was close.

He swung his rifle around and turned to face the source of the slight noise. He touched a hand to the lever of the

Winchester, ready to cock it and slide a cartridge into the firing chamber.

The hairs on the back of his neck bristled as he heard what sounded like sandpaper being rubbed across soft wood. A shape, a dark blob, rose out of the emptiness a few yards in front of him and he saw a flash of silver as moonlight glanced off the blade of a knife. He dropped the rifle and drew his own knife in the fraction of a second he had before the Kiowa charged straight at him, his knife held high as if to plunge it down into his chest.

Slocum went into a fighting crouch and stepped to one side. He smelled the paint on the brave's face, the grease in his hair, the sweat on his body. The knife in the Kiowa's hand came slashing down, striking empty air in the spot where Slocum had stood. The brave's feet clicked the rifle and it slid a few inches to one side.

Slocum lashed out with his knife, a large Bowie, sharp as a razor on both sides of the blade, but the Kiowa bent double and, like a cat, hopped to one side. The Bowie knife carved a slice of empty air and Slocum danced to one side as the Kiowa bent low and came at him again, this time with his knife held just below his waist.

Slocum sidestepped and kicked at the knife hand of the Kiowa. His boot struck the man's wrist, but the Kiowa did not drop the knife. Instead, he whirled and dashed at Slocum, slashing from side to side. The two men grappled and Slocum felt a sharp stab in the upper part of his leg. He groaned in pain and wrestled the Kiowa to the ground as hot blood seeped from his wound and soaked his trouser leg.

The two men rolled on the rocky ground, each trying to stab the other. The Kiowa was as silent as stone, but Slocum grunted with the effort. Finally, he slammed his left arm into the brave's throat, knocking his head back. Slocum saw an opening and struck with the big Bowie, aiming straight at the soft spot beneath the Kiowa's rib cage.

He felt the knife puncture flesh and slide into the man's

stomach. Air escaped from the wound and Slocum wrenched his knife upward, toward the man's heart. He heard the scrape of the blade on a rib and the Kiowa made a huffing noise and spasmed as the blade sliced through veins and arteries, the tip of it ramming into the bottom of the man's heart. It felt to Slocum as if he were striking a sponge. He turned the blade and raked it sideways through the lungs on the man's right side. More air escaped through the large gash in the Kiowa's midsection. He kicked both legs, gasped, and then lay still. Blood gushed from the large opening in his stomach and then ceased as his heart stopped beating.

Slocum ripped off the bandanna he wore around his neck and wrapped it just above the wound in his leg. He pulled it tight and tied it as a lassitude crept into his mind. He felt faint and stood up on shaky legs.

The earth spun around him, and he felt as if he was going to faint.

He wiped the bloody blade of his knife on his trousers and slipped it back into its sheath. He staggered toward his rifle and bent over to pick it up. The rifle quivered beneath his blurred gaze as his fingers grasped the barrel.

The pain in his leg rippled up to his brain and shrieked with a blinding loudness that made him stumble toward the adobe, using only his sense of direction as stars whirled in the sky and the moon danced like a bouncing ball overhead.

A shadow emerged out of a clump of sage and started toward him. He saw the lone feather sprouting from the man's scalp, a white flash against the sky. John worked the lever on his Winchester and fired from the hip as the man rushed toward him. He caught a glimpse of the war club in the Kiowa's hand as he was drawing it back to hurl it at him.

Slocum squeezed the trigger when the brave was less than ten feet from him. The rifle roared and spat flame and lead from the muzzle. The Kiowa stumbled to a stop two feet from Slocum. There was a stain on his breastplate, a stain that widened before he fell forward. The war club fell from his hand as he hit the ground with a dull thud.

Slocum heard a startled scream from somewhere near the adobe.

He staggered past the fallen body of the Kiowa, the smoke from his rifle clinging to his nostrils. The smell of exploded powder was strong and helped to clear his head for a moment.

"John," Melissa called. "Was that you?"

"Yeah," he said and the stars collapsed over his head. The moon melted and he felt himself falling into a dark pit. He struggled to stay on his feet, but the earth pulled him down. He slid a half foot when he hit the ground and the darkness entered his brain and shut off his senses as if an iron door had slammed shut.

He floated somewhere between light and dark, lost to the world, deaf to all sound, blind to all that had been visible, and frozen in some timeless limbo that existed between life and death.

5

Slocum awoke with the sound and sting of a hand slapping his face. He opened his eyes and saw a wavery image of Melissa's face just above his.

"John, John!" she shrieked. "Wake up!"

"I'm awake," he croaked. He felt light-headed and woozy. Melissa reared back and stopped slapping him.

"My God, what happened?" she said as Slocum struggled to sit up. He felt a sharp pain in his left leg. The pain vanquished most of the shadows in his mind. His focus returned and he remembered all that had happened to him. The stars settled down into fixed points of light. The moon steadied and glowed against the velvet black sky.

"Long story," he said as he pulled himself to his feet. Melissa picked up his rifle and handed it to him.

"You're hurt," she said.

"A scratch, but I've got to lie down and put a compress on my wound."

"Can you walk to the adobe?"

"Yes, but stay close. I might need to steady myself. My left leg feels numb."

She glanced down at his leg and gasped.

"You're covered in blood."

"Dried blood, I hope."

She touched the bloody trousers with delicate fingers.

"It's wet, but drying, I think."

He made out the dim outlines of the adobe and limped toward it. Melissa held one elbow with her hand and walked with him. He went inside and sat down on his tarp, which was part of his bedroll. He removed one of his spurs while Melissa looked on. A shaft of moonlight gave him enough light to see. It shimmered with dust motes.

Slocum took the spur and untied the knot in his bandanna. Then he placed the tong of the spur in the center and retied the knot. As Melissa looked on, he twisted the spur, shutting off the blood flow to his wound. He had no idea how deep it was, or if the Kiowa's blade had struck an artery, but he knew that if it had, he would probably be dead by now. That leg artery could drain a man's blood in a few minutes.

"That's a tourniquet, right?" Melissa said.

"Just to make sure the bleeding stops."

"It must hurt a lot," she said.

"Some. Not much. I might be in shock."

"Oh, no," she breathed, then she knelt beside him, worried.

"We'll see," he said, and lay down.

"I'll bring your blanket in, John."

"I feel pretty hot right now. You keep it."

She stood up, brushed dirt off her dress.

"I'm not leaving you alone. Do you want a drink of water?"

"When you get time," he said, and there was a weariness in his voice that she detected.

"I'll be right back," she said.

"I'm not going anywhere." His voice was weak, he knew, and there was a throbbing pain in his leg right under the knot in his bandanna. The spur gleamed silver in the beam of moonlight.

Melissa was not right back. She was gone for several minutes. Slocum loosened the tourniquet, waited five minutes, then tightened it again. He felt the cloth of the bandanna, and noted that it was drying out where it covered the wound. That was a good sign.

He heard the patter of footsteps outside the decrepit adobe and, a moment later, a rustle of cloth. Then Melissa walked in with the blanket all balled up in her arms.

"I saw him," she said. "I saw the Injun you killed. He's plumb dead, but still scary with all that paint on his face."

She unfurled the blanket and placed it over Slocum's legs, pulled it up to just below his chin.

"Curiosity killed the cat," he said.

"I—I was curious. I couldn't help it. I had to know. I had to see for myself."

"There's another dead one out there. I found a spring with a pump. There's fresh water to be had."

"Water," she said, and picked up one of the wooden canteens. She knelt beside Slocum and took the cork out of the canteen. She tilted the wooden flask and held it to his lips. Slocum drank and nearly choked when she lifted the canteen bottom and more water poured through the spout.

He spluttered and gasped for breath as water entered his windpipe.

"Oh, I'm so sorry, John. I didn't mean to . . ."

He waved her away.

"It's all right," he said.

As she watched, he loosened the tourniquet again, removed the spur.

He reached in his pocket and drew out a box of wooden matches.

"Here, strike one of these so I can get a look at this wound."

He unwrapped the bandanna and exposed the wound.

Melissa lit a match and held it over the slice in his pants. He pulled on both sides of the fabric and exposed the wound under the glare of the match flame. The blood had coagulated and there was a thin patina over the slit.

The match burned her fingers and she shook it out.

"It looks okay to me," he said. "If it doesn't get infected, it ought to heal up pretty fast."

"Do you want me to light another match?"

"No. You might burn your fingers off," he said.

"Well, you don't need to be so critical. I wasn't looking at the match. I was looking at the wound in your leg. Do you have another pair of trousers?"

"No. I travel light. But I've got a needle and thread to patch it in the morning."

"I can sew it for you," she said.

"I've got to find that creek, though. I want to pack this with mud and some moss so it will heal quick."

"You can do that?"

"I've done it before," he said.

"Were you in the war?" she asked.

"Sort of."

She cocked her head in a quizzical pose, but Slocum didn't elaborate.

"I know," she said. "I ask too many questions."

"Can you handle a rifle or a six-gun, Melissa?"

"Yes. My daddy taught me to shoot. He taught all us kids to shoot both rifle and pistol."

"I need some shut-eye. Keep that rifle handy. It's ready to shoot. Just pull the hammer back. I left it on half cock."

"I'll stand guard," she said.

"You'd better stay inside with me. At least you'll have some wall between you and whoever might try to sneak up on us."

"Yes, I think that's a good idea. I'll get my bag and find a place to sit or lie down."

Slocum closed his eyes and threw an arm across his face to block the starlight and the glow of the moon.

He was asleep by the time Melissa came back with her carpetbag. She set it down and picked up the Winchester, held it to her shoulder. It was not as heavy as the Henry her father had owned and made her shoot. She looked down the barrel at the front sight and swung the rifle in a slow arc to get the feel of it.

Then she sat down in a corner after inspecting it with her hands to see if there was anything alive there. She leaned back and looked at the sleeping Slocum. He was a shadow beneath the blanket, but at least he did not snore. Soon, she closed her eyes and dozed off, the rifle in her lap, one hand on the stock, the other on the barrel.

An hour later, Melissa awoke with a start. The rifle had slid from her lap and was lying on the floor. A large rat sat on the stock, its tiny eyes gleaming like jewels. Melissa stifled a scream and drew back against the corners of the wall. The rat's whiskers twitched and it sat up, rubbed its forepaws together. She eased one leg around and raised it. She kicked at the rat and it squealed as it scurried away, its tail wagging a meaningless semaphore, its fur bristling under the shine of moonlight.

Melissa rose to her feet and shuddered as she thought of how close the rat had been to her. It must have pulled the rifle off her lap, she thought, or sat on the stock so that the rifle tilted and slid from her grasp.

She looked at Slocum asleep on the floor and walked over to him. His blanket had slid off and was lying rumpled next to him. She lay down beside him, snuggled up close, and pulled the blanket over her legs and onto Slocum. She quivered against him, terrified that the rat might return and crawl under the blanket. She snuggled even closer to Slocum and lay her arm across his chest.

She closed her eyes but could not sleep. She kept thinking

about the rat and then she thought about Slocum, how close he was, how warm he felt. One of her breasts touched his arm and she felt the nipple harden without any willingness of her own. He was a big man, and she felt safe lying next to him. She also felt stirrings in her own body and emotions. She had longed for such a man back in Illinois, a strong man who was self-sufficient and handsome.

Did such dreams really come true? she wondered.

But now, she lay next to such a man, a man who had rescued her and killed two Kiowa to protect her. She owed him something, she reasoned.

She owed him her life, for one thing.

Perhaps she owed him much more. Did she dare to make the first move? What would John Slocum think of her if she showed him affection and more? Would he treat her like a slattern and have nothing more to do with her? Or was there a tenderness in him that might make him want to hold her tight and perhaps kiss her on the lips? And where would that lead?

She reached up and touched Slocum's face. She felt the wiry bristles of his beard, stroked his chin. A small thrill coursed through her body and his stillness emboldened her.

She propped herself up on one elbow and leaned over his face. She gazed down at him, at his closed eyes, the square chin, the strong jaw, and became overcome with a rising passion that she could not stem. She kissed him lightly on the lips and electricity shot through her body and stirred her loins, generated a heat between her legs that warmed her entire body.

She reached down with one hand and found the bulge in Slocum's crotch. She stroked and caressed it, felt the slow hardening as blood began to engorge his cock.

She continued to fondle his member until it grew long and hard as it lay on his abdomen. Her desire turned to lust and she crawled atop him. She lifted her dress and slid onto him, with only her panties touching his member inside his pants. She scooted back and forth, gently at first, and touched his lips with her fingers, wanting him, wanting him so badly, she could scream.

She began to gyrate her hips and she felt Slocum's hips respond, rising to meet her loins as if connected with invisible threads or sinew. He grew still harder and she pressed her pussy down on him until the fire rose to a feverish pitch.

With frantic fingers, Melissa unbuckled Slocum's belt as she arched above him. She unbuttoned his fly and exposed him. He was not wearing undershorts and his cock rose up like a mighty staff, inviting, throbbing, swollen to huge proportions.

Melissa slipped out of her panties and lowered herself onto Slocum's cock, sliding it into her steaming portal, which was slick with the oils of desire.

She sighed and his eyes flickered open. He stared at her with a startled gaze of those green eyes.

6

Slocum reached out and grasped Melissa's buttocks. She responded with quick undulations of her body and he held her tight against him as he thrust upward with his swollen cock. He burrowed deep within her and felt the quivering response as he plumbed the depths of her cunt with driving force.

"Oh, John," Melissa cooed, "it's so good. It—it's beyond belief."

"You surprised me," he said, and she bore down on him with her hips and he rose to meet her, to plumb the very depths of her womb. He pulled on her buttocks as they rose and fell. She squirmed in his embrace.

He felt a twinge of pain in his wounded leg, but it passed and he did not detect any bleeding. The wound was forgotten in the heat and passion of the moment.

"Let's get out of these duds," he growled as he fought with the cloth of her dress and blouse.

"Yes, yes," she said, and slid from him.

He removed his other boot, his trousers and shirt, while she slipped her dress from her body.

They coupled again when both were naked.

"Much better," he said. "Your skin is soft."

"I love it," she said, nearly breathless, as she lay on her back and spread her legs wide.

Slocum dipped down and slid into her. She cried out as his cock grazed her clit. Her body jumped with a sudden spasm as if an electric shock had passed through her.

She screamed softly as his cock reached its zenith and pistoned back and forth while buried deep in the folds of her sex.

A soft wind sniffed at the windows and door of the adobe, riffled through the fallen rafters, and then began to whistle as it surged through the broken-down structure.

Slocum and Melissa rose and fell to an ancient rhythm. She peppered his face with kisses, then engaged his mouth with hers. Her tongue slid between his lips and there was fire in her loins, lava in the soft pudding of her pussy. The kiss seemed to recharge her energy and she lifted her hips to meet his downward thrusts. They climbed the heights together in a gust of passion as the wind keened soft songs in the crumbling bricks of the adobe.

They sailed to the summit of their passion, and their bodies quivered with the sudden blast of twin orgasms. Melissa cried out in ecstasy as an electric thrill surged through her supple body. Slocum gasped with pleasure as he squirted his milky seed into her grasping cunt.

They floated down from the pinnacle of pleasure, sated, warm, spent.

He rolled off her pliant body and lay beside her. He reached for his shirt and fumbled for a cheroot. He pulled out a box of matches and struck one, lit the end of his smoke.

"Umm," she moaned. "Smells good."

"Want one?" he asked.

"No. I'm satisfied just lying next to you. John, you gave me so much pleasure. I—I'm truly grateful."

"The pleasure, Melissa, was mostly mine. You're a lovely woman and there is no end to your womanly gifts."

The wind increased to gale velocity and howled through the rafters. Pieces of wood became airborne and the two lovers had to duck as they were donning their clothes.

"We'd better head for the canyon until this blow is over," Slocum said.

"All right. I'll get my bag."

"No, just leave everything here. I'll lead Ferro and we'll walk into the wind."

"Are we coming back here?" she asked as she brushed her hair into some semblance of uniformity.

"I want to water my horse and fill the canteens. This wind is going to play hob with those tracks."

The two walked out of the disheveled adobe and Slocum untied Ferro. He left the saddle, saddlebags, and bedroll behind as they walked to the canyon. They braced themselves against the roaring West Texas wind and leaned into it.

Melissa said something, but her words were lost to Slocum. The wind snatched them away as soon as they left her mouth.

They descended into the blackness of Palo Duro Canyon and immediately were able to stand upright for the first time since they had left their woebegone shelter.

"Ahhh," Melissa breathed as her fingers combed through her tangled hair.

"Let's find a spot to sit down," he said. "Maybe we can catch a little shut-eye before morning."

"Is this wind ever going to let up?" she asked.

They could hear it roar above them like a wild river.

"It should lessen by morning," he said.

"You don't sound very sure about that."

"I'm not. I've seen it blow like this for days with little letup."

They found a spot next to the canyon wall. Slocum lay his rifle down next to Melissa and tied Ferro to a sturdy bush a few yards away.

"I'll feed you in the morning, boy," he said to the horse.

Slocum sat down and moved the rifle to his other side, so he could nudge up against Melissa for warmth. It was chilly, but at least they were out of the wind.

"Can you sleep?" he asked.

"If you put your arm around me and hold me real tight," she said.

He put his arm around her. She nestled her head in the hollow beneath his shoulder and closed her eyes. Slocum set his hat down and leaned back against the cold wall of the canyon. He had slept in worse places, he thought. He closed his eyes and listened to the keening of the wind as it flowed overhead. Only an occasional gust dipped down into the canyon, ruffling a few plants and dislodging a rock or two with the subsequent rattle of sliding sand.

He thought of the two dead Kiowa and the spring with its rusted pump. It would be hell tracking those kidnapped women, his horses, the Kiowa, and the man called Scud. He didn't know of any nearby towns, but then it had been a long time since he had been in that desolate part of Texas. In those days, he knew, towns sprang up and then were abandoned, became ghost towns. Some of them were no more than rubble, what with the strong winds, the flash floods, and the twisters that often desecrated the landscape.

But he was determined to rescue the three captive women and retrieve his horses.

They've got to be going somewhere, he reasoned, somewhere near this long canyon.

He slept and dreamed of Kiowa and horses and the shadowy man called Scud.

7

Slocum awoke before dawn while the canyon still basked in darkness. The wind had died down, slid away during the night like a vanquished banshee. There was a chill in the air. Ferro whickered softly as Slocum stood up and walked away to relieve himself. He could smell Melissa's musk on his body and the smell was good and comforting. She lay in a heap at the foot of the wall, sound asleep.

He lit a cheroot and waited for the dawn he knew would come. He looked up at the wall behind Melissa and saw the first tinge of pink, a thin line along the rocky rim that slowly crawled downward.

He jostled Melissa to awaken her. Her eyes came open and there was a look of bewilderment in them that soon vanished when she saw him standing there, looking down at her.

"Morning," he said. "The rosy fingers of dawn are touching the land above this canyon."

He helped her to her feet. She brushed herself off, and patted her hair.

"Oh, I'll never get my hair straight," she said.

"Just hope you don't have sand fleas in it," he smiled.

She scrubbed her hair with both hands and glared at him.

He walked over to Ferro and untied him.

"Let's get up to the sunlight," he said. "It'll warm up soon and you can comb your hair out while we tend to business."

"Tend to business?"

"Yes. I aim to rescue those three gals and get my horses back from those redskins."

"I dreamed," she said. "I dreamed I was in Saint Louis at a fine hotel and there was a large bed and a window that looked out over the Mississippi. I went out and down to the lobby, which was resplendent with gold and red brocade and crystal chandeliers. I wandered around for a long time. I couldn't find my room, and I walked up and down elegant staircases and saw people dressed in finery, and I never could find my floor or my room. Then you woke me up."

Slocum laughed.

"I've had dreams like that, only I wasn't in a fine hotel, but a weather-beaten old whorehouse, and the women were ugly and fat, and my room looked out over a hog pen with an old man pouring slop into their troughs."

Melissa laughed and they climbed up out of the canyon. Slocum carried his rifle in his left hand and led Ferro with the other.

The land was painted a rosy pink, with splotches of orange and bright red on the Indian paintbrushes. Yellow butterflies danced in the sun like tiny sailing ships, and a quail piped its plaintive call. The rocks seemed to glow a bright brown, and a gentle breeze jostled the sage and the Spanish bayonets.

Slocum saddled up Ferro and tied his rolled-up bedroll behind the cantle after he draped the saddlebags over the horse's rump. Melissa changed clothes, exchanging her long dress for a pair of homely duck trousers and a pale blue chambray shirt. She carried her carpetbag outside and handed it to Slocum. He looked at her and flashed a wry smile.

"You know, in some towns, they hang women for wearing men's trousers."

"They're my brother's. He gave them to me in case I had to paint or do farm chores where I was going. I thought they would be more comfortable."

"Well, you can't hide who you are," Slocum said. "I know there's a woman in those trousers."

Melissa blushed as Slocum took her bag and tied it snug against the bedroll. He picked up the canteens, sheathed his rifle after inserting a fresh cartridge in the magazine, and helped her climb up onto her perch atop the carpetbag.

They rode past the dead Kiowa as Melissa clung to him, and on to the water pump, where the other Indian lay dead, his blood dried to a dark rust.

Slocum filled the two wooden canteens, let Ferro drink after he fed him a hatful of corn and oats he had in his saddlebags. He loosened the cinches then tightened them up again when Ferro had drunk his fill.

"Now where?" Melissa asked as Slocum settled back in the saddle.

"That cut on my leg sealed up during the night, so I don't need much leaves or mold on it. I'm going to see if I can pick up any tracks after that hellish blow last night."

They rode along the canyon, which began to widen gradually the farther south they went. He saw no tracks for a long time, but he figured the band of Kiowa and their captive horses and women had stayed in the canyon overnight. There were no landmarks and no signs of habitation anywhere in range of his sight. Later, they came to a game trail leading down into the canyon and that's when he spotted fairly fresh tracks emerging from the canyon and heading south.

Even Melissa saw that the ground had changed.

"Are those the tracks you're looking for?" she asked.

"Yep. They came out of that canyon about two hours ago. Must have bedded down for the night, out of the wind."

Melissa sighed.

"Well, it's flat out here. You can see for miles."

"Yes, you can see pretty far, but there could be Kiowa waiting in some gully or shallow arroyo. We'll see."

An hour later, Melissa, dozing against Slocum's back, listened to her stomach growl.

"I'm hungry," she said.

"I've got some hardtack and jerky in my saddlebag," he said. "I could gnaw on some dried beef myself."

"There are no shade trees."

"We can sit under Ferro here and he'll give us shade."

That's what they did some fifteen minutes later as the sun stood well above the eastern horizon, its fiery disk glowing like the bowels of a blast furnace. They nibbled on their simple food and swallowed water from one of the canteens. The water was warm, but not yet hot, and there was a slight breeze crawling along the ground. They sweated, but the flicks of Ferro's tail were like a servant's fan and served to cool them some.

Ferro's hide was streaked with sweat and there were bloody streaks where the flies had nipped him. They rode on and then Slocum saw what he had dreaded seeing. The tracks were all moiled in a rough circle, and as he rode farther on, he saw four sets of horse tracks that were made by iron shoes, flanked by two sets of tracks from unshod ponies. The other tracks continued on to the south, but his horses were heading east.

He reined up Ferro for a moment and pulled a cheroot from his shirt pocket. He struck a wooden match and lighted the cigar, returned the matchbox to his pocket, and drew smoke into his lungs.

"Resting?" Melissa said.

"Thinking," Slocum replied.

"About what?"

"My horses have split from Scud's bunch."

She looked down at the ground, but could make no sense of what she saw, just a maze of tracks.

"What are you going to do?" she asked, and he detected a note of fear in her voice.

Slocum lifted his left foot out of the stirrup and cocked his leg around the pommel so that he was facing sideways.

"I have to make a decision," he said.

"You mean . . ." She hesitated.

"Go ahead and say it," he said.

"You're wondering whether to follow Scud or go after your horses."

He smiled and blew a ragged smoke ring into the air. It wobbled like the ghost of a doughnut, then shredded in the breeze.

"The businessman in me says to go after the horses," he said.

"But . . ."

"But the missionary in me says I should follow Scud and rescue those three gals."

Melissa didn't laugh. Instead, she frowned.

"Which is the stronger?" she asked. "The missionary or the businessman?"

Slocum took a long minute to answer as he worked a ball of smoke around in his mouth then let it seep slowly through his lips.

"It's an easy choice," he said as he swung his leg back down and slipped his boot into the stirrup.

"Easy?"

"Yes. Horses are a dime a dozen. Kidnapped women are as rare as diamonds in a slaughterhouse."

"So, you'll go after Scud and free my friends," she said.

"Yep. I'm just wondering where those two Kiowa are taking my horses. Is there a camp out there where they will join up with their own kind, or a ranch I can't see where they'll sell the horses for food, money, or whiskey?"

She peered off to the east, shading her eyes with a flattened hand.

"I can't see anything out there."

"Texas is a big place," he said.

"Where do you think that Scud is taking the women he kidnapped?"

"Must be a town somewhere along this canyon is all I can figure. I haven't been down this way in a long while, and then it was only once and I didn't go very far."

"What were you doing here before?" she asked.

"I rode with a Texas Ranger after a couple of escaped prisoners who murdered a woman in Amarillo, raped her daughter, and cut her son's throat with a knife. There was a big reward out for those two sonsofbitches and I was deputized."

"And did you find them?"

"Yes, we found them, asked them to surrender."

"Did they?"

"No, they threw down on us, rode into the canyon. We blew them both out of their saddles and left their carcasses to rot. It was hellish hot and we didn't give a damn about carrying them back to Amarillo."

"So, you didn't get the reward," she said.

"Oh, we got it, all right. We took their gun belts, rifles, and shirts back with us and the judge saw the bullet holes and the dried blood on their shirts and awarded us each two hundred and fifty dollars."

"So, you're a bounty hunter," she said.

"Sometimes."

They rode on into the late afternoon, following the tracks.

The tracks descended down a narrow defile back into the canyon. Slocum guided Ferro down into the wide fissure, then followed tracks back up another defile onto the western side of the canyon. The tracks headed south and west.

Just before the sun fell behind the horizon, they came to a wide road. The road was marred by wagon tracks and horses' hooves and what appeared to be a few cattle tracks.

"Funny to find a road out here," Melissa said.

"I think I've seen that road before. Not here, but back where the canyon begins to the north. I wondered where such a road would lead."

"And now you know."

"Not quite, but there's something up ahead."

He pointed and Melissa leaned to the side to look around him.

Some two hundred yards away, the road split into two branches. In the crook of the two roads there was a pole with a board nailed to it.

"What is it?" she asked.

"It's a road sign, looks like," he said.

They rode up to it. The board was cut at both ends to points.

Someone had painted the sign in bright red. One, pointing east, read: PALO DURO CANYON. The other legend, pointing west, read: POLVO.

"Polvo?" Melissa said. "What does that mean?"

"It's probably a town or a settlement, I figure."

"Polvo," she said. "Funny name for a town."

"It means 'dust' in Spanish," Slocum said.

"Huh?"

"Dust," he said. "Probably a right-fitting name for a town way out here. Anyway, that's where the tracks lead and that's where we're going to go."

They rode toward Polvo, toward the unknown, as the sun drew long shadows across the land in its descent beyond the rim of their world. There was just a trace of coolness in the breeze that blew out of the west. Ferro whinnied and Slocum knew that he had scented water somewhere ahead of them.

Dust and water, he thought.

Not so strange a mixture out here in this desolate land, where they might die of either one if he stayed long enough.

8

They rode into the setting sun and into the puddles of their own shadows.

Presently, they heard a rumbling and then saw, silhouetted against the western sky, a wagon pulled by two horses and carrying two men.

The driver of the wagon hauled in on the reins and stopped the horses.

"Howdy," he said to Slocum and Melissa.

"Howdy yourself," Slocum said. "Where you headed?"

"Back to Amarillo. We make two trips a week to Polvo."

"What kind of town is Polvo?" Slocum asked.

The other man answered the question. He was in his forties and wore a black derby, a string tie, and an armband.

"New and wide open," the man said. "I reckon that's where you two are headed."

"What do you mean by 'wide open'?" Slocum asked, directing his question to the derby-hatted one.

"If you're goin' there, you'll see. Big saloon, bright new gamblin' tables, glitter gals. Fact is Scudder just brought in three more pretties he promised to put on display tomorrow night."

"Any Kiowa in town?"

The driver, who wore a battered Montana hat with a high crown and a deep crease, shook his head.

"No Injuns that I ever saw," he said. "Well, we got to get crackin'. Scud wants us to haul in more liquor and feed sacks on our next run."

"Have a good trip back to Amarillo," Slocum said, and touched two fingers to the brim of his hat in a farewell salute.

"Nice hotel there, too," Derby Hat said, "and they're puttin' up another one, even bigger."

"What's the big attraction to Polvo?" Slocum asked as the team started to move off under the snapping of the reins.

"Scud claims gold and silver in the sand hills," the man said, his voice trailing off as the wagon rumbled away.

The two men waved as Melissa and Slocum watched them ride off into the twilight.

"Gold and silver," Melissa said.

"Don't believe everything you hear," Slocum said. "But now we know who's running the saloon, if not the whole town."

"Scud," she said.

"Short for Scudder, I reckon. That man called him Scudder."

"And those three women . . ."

"Probably your friends," he said.

They rode on and came upon another sign. This one said POLVO in block letters. Underneath the name, the sign had originally read, POP. 45, but the number had been crossed out with a slash of paint and replaced by 72, which had also been struck out and still another number had been painted on: 122.

"The town is growing," Slocum said.

"I wonder how often they put up a new number," Melissa said as they rode on.

"I don't know, but it's still a small town and no good reason to be here."

"You think Scud—"

"Is as crooked as a snake," Slocum said, finishing her sentence.

In the dimming light, Slocum noticed that the unshod pony tracks had peeled off and headed south, leaving only the tracks of the shod horses beneath the impressions of the wagon wheels and the team pulling it.

"It seems the Kiowa didn't go into town," Slocum said.

"How do you know?"

"I just saw sign that the Kiowa had left Scud and his captives."

"What do you make of that?" she asked.

"Like the man said, there aren't any Kiowa in town. They served their purpose for Scud and he sent them away."

"It's all so very mysterious, John," she said.

"White men have been exploiting the red man for a long time, Melissa. They buy the Indians cheap with whiskey or guns, knives, and worthless trinkets. It's nothing new."

"It's horrible," she said, and then they both were silent as they saw the graying structures of a town loom up ahead of them.

They entered the three-street town as the sun was setting. There were no lights on any of the streets, but there was an orange glow coming from two buildings on the main street. The lamps threw a pool of light on a bare street and daubed a few saddle horses and a cart or two with a pale patina of yellowish light.

Most of the houses they had seen were clapboard structures, but there were a few adobes, and the occasional false front attached to an adobe building.

"They built this town cheap," Slocum remarked.

"There isn't much to it," Melissa said as they rode up to the hotel, with its tall false front and a sign proclaiming it as THE EXCELSIOR. Two doors down was a saloon, with its false front and a long adobe building hiding behind the clapboard.

The saloon was the Desert Rose, and they could hear banjo, guitar, and fiddle music over the sound of a snare and bass drum. Across the street there was a small building tagged as POLVO BANK, and next to that was a clapboard building that bore a painted sign on its door that read: GOLDEN KEY ASSAY OFFICE.

"Are we going in here?" Melissa asked as Slocum pulled up to the hitch rail. There were three horses tied up there, each bearing the same brand, a Lazy S. One of the brands appeared to have been overlaid on an earlier one with a running iron. The rifle scabbards were empty and none of them had saddlebags or bedrolls.

"We need sleep and a soft bed," he said. "I'm going to look around. Maybe they serve grub in here. Are you hungry?"

"Famished," she said.

He untied her carpetbag and the two walked on loose dirt to the entrance and entered the lobby. As soon as they entered, they could smell cooked food—meat and potatoes, vegetables. There was a room off the lobby where they could hear the clinking of glasses, plates, and silverware.

"I'll get us a room," he said.

"Just one room?"

"I don't think your reputation will be damaged if we share a single room," he said. "Not in this one-horse town."

She laughed self-consciously.

"I—I guess not. After all, I don't know anyone here and you probably don't either."

"We'll see who you know," he said, and walked to the desk, where an aging male clerk stood with a green shade attached to his forehead.

"Yes, sir, a room for the night? Or will you stay longer? I'm James Parsons, the night clerk. I just came on."

"Yes, one night. One soft bed."

"First or second floor? We have two stories, you know."

"Second floor is fine. Toward the back, if you don't mind."

Parsons turned and looked at the keys dangling from brass hooks on a board.

"Number 220 is at the back, down at the end of the hall. Not much of a view there."

"That'll be fine," Slocum said.

"A dollar fifty," Parsons said.

Slocum pulled out two one-dollar bills and laid them on the counter.

"Keep the change for yourself, Parsons," he said.

Parsons grinned and scooped up the bills. He opened a drawer, placed them inside, and extracted a four-bit piece that he put in his pocket. He turned a ledger around and shoved it toward Slocum.

"If you would, sir, please sign our guest book."

Slocum wrote: *Mr. & Mrs. Joe Wilson.* It seemed as good a name as any, and besides, he was still a wanted man, accused of a murder he didn't commit in Georgia. He was not free with his name, since wanted dodgers had a way of traveling across country and turning up in small towns. Even new ones.

Parsons turned back to the key board and took down a large skeleton key with a tag that bore the number 220 written in black ink.

"Here you are, Mr., ah, Wilson," Parsons said as he read the register upside down.

Slocum took the key and pocketed it.

"I see your wife is waiting for you. The dining room is open until eleven p.m. Enjoy your stay, Mr. Wilson."

"Thanks, Mr. Parsons," Slocum said, and walked toward Melissa, who was staring through the wide doorway into the dining hall.

They walked in, arm in arm, like a proper married couple. Slocum leaned down to whisper into her ear.

"Give me a sign if you see Scud in here," he said. "Or your friends."

"I will," she said.

A waiter came up to them. He wasn't wearing fancy clothes, just denim trousers, a small apron, and a white shirt and string tie. His hair was black and heavily pomaded. It glistened in the flickering light from the candle-laden chandeliers. It was not an elegant place, Slocum thought, but it was clean enough, and the smell of food was overpowering.

"A table for two," the waiter said. "My name is Horace and I will be taking your order."

He led them to a table and pointed to a sign above two batwing doors.

"That is our bill of fare for this evening," he said.

Slocum read the sparse sign as they sat down. Horace pulled out Melissa's chair and seated her.

"We'll have the beefsteak, boiled potatoes, green beans, and biscuits," he said.

"We have water and spirits," Horace said. "Wine and beer that are both room temperature."

"I'll have water," Melissa said.

"Beer for me," Slocum said.

"I'll be back with your order shortly," Horace said.

Slocum looked around the room. There were two men seated at one table forking up food to their mouths and talking out of the sides of their mouths. A portly man and a woman sat at another table. Three men sat in the center of the room, their faces mottled with dust, their hats tipped back from sweat-laden foreheads. They wore worker's shirts and dust-clogged trousers, work boots that bore scars and stains. They were not speaking much, but just shoveling food into their maws as if they hadn't had a hot meal in weeks.

"Recognize anybody here?" Slocum asked, his voice low and confidential in tone.

Melissa stared at the other diners quickly then met Slocum's gaze.

"No, I'm afraid not," she said.

"Didn't expect we'd find Scud in here treating his captive women to a good meal."

"Surely he'll feed them," she said.

"Yeah, I'm sure he will. Gruel or swill, likely."

"That's terrible," she said.

"Look, Melissa, Scud and his band of Kiowa killed two men just so he could grab your friends. He would have taken you, too, if he had found you. To me, the man is an animal. Even though I've never met Scud, I know what kind of a man he is."

"Yes, I suppose you're right. I just hope he treats my friends halfway decently."

"Don't count on it," Slocum said.

One of the men at the far table stood up and walked toward the table where Slocum and Melissa sat. He was wearing a gun belt and the holster was slung low, so that his hand could dangle close to the butt.

As he approached, Slocum saw that he was wearing a tin star on his vest. As he drew closer, Slocum read the word *Sheriff* on his badge. He looked ready to fight. He was a man with a ruddy, windblown complexion, a neck that bore streaks of dirt in its folds. He had on worn pinstripe trousers and his shirt was as yellow as butter. He wore a tightly wound bandanna around his neck, as red as a Texas sunset.

Melissa looked up at the man as he came to a stop a few feet from their table.

She gasped and brought a hand to her mouth. She looked as if she were in shock.

"Stranger," the man said, "don't I know you from somewhere?"

The sheriff's right hand floated above his pistol grip as if he was ready to draw at a moment's notice.

Slocum's eyes narrowed and his jaw tightened as he stared at the man with a penetrating gaze, his hand inching down his side to the butt of his Colt.

The room seemed to go dead still. There was not a sound from the diners. They all looked over at Slocum's table as if expecting some unknown event to occur.

9

Slocum's hand opened and closed to grip the butt of his
Colt .45. The man with the badge standing next to their table
looked dangerous, as if he was spoiling for a gunfight.

And Melissa had reacted to him in a strange way.

In a calm voice, Slocum replied to the sheriff's question.

"No, sir, we haven't met and I have no business with the
law in this town. Not yet."

The sheriff acted as if Slocum had slapped his face. His
jaw line stretched and tautened and his lips curled in an
ominous snarl.

"I've seen you somewhere before," the sheriff said. "Or
maybe your picture on a wanted dodger. What's your name?"

"Wilson," Slocum said. His grip tightened on the butt of
his pistol, and he pulled it a half inch. His hand was under
the table and could not be seen by anyone in the dining
room.

"Wilson, eh? It don't ring no bell. But you might be using
an alias."

The accusation hovered between the two men like a black cloud ready to burst into a stabbing flash of lightning.

"Is this how you treat newcomers to Polvo?" Slocum asked. "And I haven't heard your name yet, Sheriff."

"The name's Oren Scudder if that's any business of yours."

Slocum heard a soft gasp from Melissa. He did not take his gaze off Sheriff Scudder.

"It might be," Slocum said. "If you're accusing me of anything, I might want to inform a U.S. marshal or a Texas Ranger."

"You threatening me?" Scudder said.

"Take it as advice. We came in here to have supper and you're holding up our service."

"Why, you sonofabitch, I ought to run you into my jail and just check through my wanted posters."

"Back off, Scudder," Slocum said. "I want no trouble, but if you keep pushing me with your threats, I just might call you out."

"I'm just doin' my job, Mr. Wilson. Now I want to know what business you have here in Polvo."

Slocum saw that the sheriff's hand no longer seemed ready to draw down on him. Instead, the sheriff crossed both arms to assume an authoritative position as if he were bossing a chain gang down in Georgia.

"I'm a horse trader," Slocum said. "Just scouting the territory."

"This is a mining town, Wilson. We got plenty of horses and ain't sellin' none of them."

"Fine. I'll look around a few days, then ride on, if that's all right with you."

The sheriff didn't seem to know that he was being tested. He thrust his jaw out in a belligerent manner as if trying to regain lost ground.

"Make it a short stay, Wilson. You don't look like you fit in here."

Slocum nodded as if in compliance, but he really wanted the sheriff to leave before one of them opened the ball.

Scudder harrumphed and turned on his heel, walked back to his table. He and his partner conversed for a few seconds, then both stole glances at Slocum and Melissa.

Melissa let out a sigh.

"That wasn't your Scud," Slocum said.

"No, but that man could be his twin. The resemblance is amazing."

"Maybe Sheriff Scudder is Scud's twin," Slocum said.

"Well, they're brothers. That's obvious."

The waiter brought water and a stein of beer, set them on the table.

"Your food will be served shortly," he said.

"Thank you, Horace," Slocum said.

The waiter left and Slocum raised the stein and toasted the sheriff and his companion before he drank. Scudder and his table companion both snorted and turned away as if they had been insulted.

Slocum sensed that this was not the last time he would hear from Scudder. The man had something stuck in his craw, and there was a good chance that he'd dig through his wanted flyers and find out that there was a reward for one John Slocum. A thousand dollars could be mighty tempting to a man like Scudder, who probably had to rely on graft to supplement his meager income.

Melissa and Slocum finished their meal. Slocum paid the bill and gave Horace a dollar. In the lobby, Slocum gave Melissa the room key.

"I'll get my rifle, saddlebags and such, and join you," he said.

"And then what?" she asked as she took the room key from him.

"I'm going to mosey on down to the saloon and see if I run into Scud or your gal friends."

"I should go with you, John."

"No, you should not go with me. No telling what I'll run into. I wouldn't be surprised if Sheriff Scudder showed up there later on."

She frowned and started for the stairs.

"It's at the end of the hall," Slocum called out after her, then went to the desk.

Parsons arose from his seat at the little desk behind the counter.

"Yes, sir, Mr. Wilson," he said. "What can I do for you?"

"I'm wondering if you have a livery stable where I could board my horse for the night."

"Yes, sir, we sure do. It's right behind the sheriff's office down the street. Scudder's Stables. Should be a stable boy there who can fix you up, store your tack, and grain your horse."

"Is the stable owned by Oren Scudder?" Slocum asked.

Parsons laughed.

"No, sir. Oren, he don't own nothin'. His brother, Jesse, owns the stable and most of the town. He even owns this hotel, matter of fact."

"No love lost between the two brothers, I gather."

"Jesse, they call him 'Scud,' he treats Oren like a hired hand, not a brother. No sir, them two don't get along except Oren's beholden to Scud for his livelihood and his job."

"I see," Slocum said. "Thanks, Mr. Parsons. I'll ride on down to the livery."

"Good evening, Mr. Wilson," Parsons said, and sat back down at his desk to bring the figures up to date.

Slocum found the stables, which were in the next block, right behind the sheriff's office as Parsons had said. The livery was a large clapboard barn with a hayloft, a tack room, water barrels, and plenty of stalls and feed troughs.

A young man came out to greet him as he dismounted.

"Good evening, sir. You want to board your horse? How long?"

"Just for the night, unless I stay longer," Slocum said.

"Be a dollar if I grain him and an extra fifteen cents if you want me to rub him down."

"All right, sonny," Slocum said.

The young man stiffened.

"My name ain't Sonny, it's Caleb," the youth said. "Caleb Lindsey."

"All right, Caleb," Slocum said as he handed the reins to the boy. He slipped off his saddlebags and drew his rifle from its sheath. "Thanks."

"You pay in advance, mister." Caleb held out his hand, palm up.

Slocum dug into his pocket and pulled out some dollar bills. He peeled off two of them and handed them to the young man.

"Give him plenty of grain and water and you can curry him. Keep the change."

Caleb looked at the two one-dollar bills and his eyes went wide.

"Gawley," he said. "Thanks, mister. I'll comb him up real good."

"See you in the morning maybe," Slocum said.

"Oh, I get off before sunup, sir. But Lew Ralston will be here to take care of you. He's the day man."

Slocum walked back to the hotel carrying his rifle and saddlebags. He climbed the stairs and walked down the long hall to Room 220. The door was locked. He tapped on it and Melissa opened the door.

"Oh, John, I'm so glad you're back."

She was plainly distraught, and he set his saddlebags down and leaned his rifle against the dresser. She had a lamp burning atop a night table and the bed was turned down. She had opened a window, and a light breeze was blowing the curtains to and fro.

"Something wrong?" he asked.

She stumbled into his arms. Her body was shaking. He squeezed her tight, then let her go.

"He was here," she said. "He came up here and just walked right in. Him and that other man."

"Who was here?" he asked.

"Sheriff Scudder and his deputy, a man named Barney Fisk."

"What did they want?" he asked as he pulled a chair out from the center table and sat down. He sailed his hat across the room and it landed atop his saddlebags.

"The sheriff offered me a job, I think."

"You think?"

"He said that a pretty girl like me could make a lot of money working at the Desert Rose."

"The saloon," he said.

"Yes. He said it was a saloon and gaming house. Only he called it a 'gambling salon' as if it was real ritzy."

"And did he tell you what you would be doing on this job?" Slocum asked.

"He—he made it sound like something special. He told me that I'd get to wear pretty dresses and that a Mexican woman would do my hair and make me up every night. He said all I had to do was be sociable, serve drinks to the gamblers, and maybe dance with some of the patrons."

"And you bought his bill of goods?"

"Sheriff Scudder said that I would get a regular salary and gratuities. He said that I could earn a lot of money. He also said that I would be furnished room and board."

Slocum snorted and fished a cheroot from his pocket. He didn't light it, but stuck it in his mouth and began to worry it back and forth, nibbling on the tip.

"What?" she said. "Whatever are you thinking, John Slocum? It sounded like a perfectly good employment offer. Pretty clothes and a hairdresser, gratuities, salary, and free lodging and meals."

Slocum jerked the cheroot from his mouth as Melissa sat down in the other chair, a look of perfect innocence on her face.

"That's about the same offer you'd get from the warden at Yuma Prison or Huntsville," he said.

"Why, whatever do you mean, John?"

"I mean the sheriff offered you a job as a glitter gal at the saloon. You'd be a soiled dove, a lady of the night. Free bed, yes, with some drunken bastard wallowing all over you every night and leaving you a dollar bill on the nightstand, a gratuity. In other words, Scudder wants his brother to hire you on as a common whore. And you would be an inmate in Scud's prison."

"Why, I never got that impression at all," she said.

"From what I found out tonight, Scud practically owns this whole town. And he knew about that wagon you were in and about women being transported to the ends of the earth. He probably set it all up so he could take your friends prisoner, put them to work as prostitutes in his castle to extract money from patrons, and make himself rich. Maybe even richer than he already is."

"That's what you think," she said as her mouth puckered up into a pout.

"I'm going up the street to have a look at the Desert Rose. I should be back sometime after midnight. I may be a little drunk, but I'll give you a full report in the morning."

"What do you expect to find out?" she asked.

"Nothing that I don't already know, Melissa. You're an innocent. You do not know the ways of the world. I'm going to give you a preview come morning."

He got up from the table, walked to his hat, and picked it up. He put it on his head and started for the door.

"John," she said.

He turned around and looked at her.

"Yes?"

"I told the sheriff that I'd take the job. Maybe I'll find my friends and maybe we'll all like the job better than marrying some stranger down in Quitaque."

Slocum glared at her.

"You poor innocent soul," he said. He jammed the cheroot back in his mouth and stormed out the door, slamming it hard behind him.

10

Slocum lit his cheroot when he walked out of the hotel. Parsons was nowhere to be seen when he crossed the lobby.

Probably gave a key to Scudder, he thought, and is hiding.

He was puffing on the little cigar when he pushed aside the batwing doors of the Desert Rose and squinted to adjust his eyesight to the splash of light and the sparkle of the crystal chandeliers with their yellow candles burning light that was reflected in overhead mirrors.

He stood there, to one side, until he could glance around the interior, scan the bar. The band was on a break, their instruments silent on wooden stands, the footlight candles blazing in small lanterns with golden glass windows.

He looked for Sheriff Scudder, but didn't see him. He walked to the end of the bar closest to the door and looked down at the men crouched over their glasses of beer, their two fingers of whiskey, smoke hanging in a blue pall over them like a thin dry cloud.

No sign of the sheriff or his deputy. No sign of any man who resembled him.

There were girls walking among the tables or sitting

down at tables, caressing the necks of fat patrons, showing their mesh-stockinged legs and ankles crossed under their short black dresses with silver trim. The women wore bright flowers in their hair, and their hair gleamed with a bright sheen under the overhead lamps.

One of the two bartenders walked down the long bar and leaned on the bar top, a towel dripping from his wide yellow sash. His sharkskin trousers were black and fit tightly over his lean frame. His shirt had ruffles on the cuffs and down the strip where the buttons fastened it. He also had a lady's garter around his arm just above the elbow. The garter was ruffled, too, and was green with black borders.

"Yes, sir, good evening," the barkeep said. "What is your pleasure?"

"Do you have any Kentucky bourbon?" Slocum asked.

"Why, we shore do. Got a shipment in from Abilene yesterday. Any particular brand suit you?"

"Old Taylor," Slocum said.

The bartender grinned. A flashy smile. Phony as a three-dollar bill, Slocum thought.

"Comin' right up," the barkeep said. He went to the back bar and produced a bottle of Old Taylor and scooped up a shot glass on his way back to where Slocum sat. He set the shot glass down and poured it full.

"Six bits," he said. "Water's ten cents extra."

"Thanks. I'll drink it straight. You can leave the bottle."

"Sure. My name's Jack," he said. "Jack Akers."

"I go by the name of Joe," Slocum said.

"Just Joe?"

"Joe Wilson. Has Sheriff Scudder come in yet?"

"Nope. You know Oren?"

"We've met." Slocum picked up his drink and looked around the room. "I was hopin' to talk to one of the gals," he said.

"I'll give Gloria the high sign," he said. "She ain't all that busy. You'll have to buy her a drink, though."

"Sure," Slocum said. "Tea at a buck a shot."

"You got it, Joe," Akers said, and walked away with a twisted little smirk on his face.

Slocum counted only three women working the tables. As he watched, one of them wended her way toward him, pausing briefly at a few tables to speak, or to pat a man on the head. She sidled up to Slocum and sat down on a stool next to him.

"Hello," she said, "I'm Gloria."

"Joe Wilson. You got a last name?"

"It's Dugan, why do you ask?"

"Sometimes a last name can tell you where a person is from, or where her parents or grandparents were born."

She laughed.

"I never heard that before. But now that I think of it, it makes sense. My grandpa was from Ireland, Limerick, Ireland. Wilson. I imagine it's English, right? From England."

"Or Scotland, or Wales," he said.

"Now you've got me guessing. Buy me a drink?"

"Sure."

He looked at the bartender. Gloria lifted a graceful hand and he poured a drink out of a tall bottle into a tall glass. Slocum laid a five-dollar bill on the bar.

"Thank you," Gloria said.

Slocum looked at her closely as she raised her glass and sipped what he took to be tea, perhaps diluted with enough whiskey to give it a smell and a slight taste were he to question what she had been served.

The heavy makeup could not completely hide her age, nor the hard years Gloria must have lived. Her hair was dyed blond, but he detected rusty red roots, and her sunken eyes were bordered by worry lines etched beneath the lids and at the sides. Her lips, too, looked shopworn and grooved by dryness and age. Her eyes were a sad blue, full of shadows that flickered like old curtains in a room full of dark secrets.

"What brings you to Polvo?" she asked, turning to look directly at Slocum.

"Oh, opportunity, I suppose," he said.

"Well, there ain't much opportunity in this burg, Mr. Wilson. Lessen you want to dig for gold or silver or sell dry goods. We got a bank, but no money to lend nobody, and the only store charges such high prices, you're better off wearin' rags."

"You didn't buy your clothes here in town," he said.

"Goodness, no. These are my working clothes, and Scud furnishes those. And most everything else around here."

She kept her voice low so that the other patrons at the bar and the barkeep couldn't hear her. She glanced around as if afraid of being overheard.

"You're not happy here?" he said.

"Happy? I ain't sad, but . . ."

"But what?"

"I think you ask too many questions, Mr. Wilson. I thought you came here to have a good time, forget your troubles, talk to a woman."

Slocum reached into his pocket and brought out a roll of greenbacks.

"How much for a few minutes of your time, Gloria?"

"You want . . ."

"Whatever you're selling," he said as he noticed her eyes fixed on the roll of bills. He held them close to his pocket, under the bar and out of sight of anyone but her, riffling them so that she could see some of the numbers.

"I have a room upstairs," she said. "For a sawbuck you can have an hour with me."

"Fair enough. You lead the way."

She reached into her bodice and pulled out a small skeleton key. She dangled it in front of Slocum.

"First, you pay, then you get my key. I'll join you in about five minutes."

Slocum peeled off a ten-dollar bill and slipped it to Gloria.

She handed him the key, which was on a little silk lanyard.

"Number 4," she said. "Lamp is lit. You make yourself comfortable and I'll see you in five minutes."

Slocum tossed down his drink after he took the key and left a couple of bills on the bar. Then he walked back to the stairs. He climbed them and found himself in a dimly lit hallway. The numbers were plain enough. He opened the door to Room 4 and entered.

There was a large bed at one end of the room, and a table on which sat a bottle of cheap whiskey and two glasses. There was also a small vase with small red and blue flowers in it. There was a wardrobe and a small dresser.

The room reeked of perfume, lilacs, he thought, or perhaps jasmine. A tall candle stood in a pewter holder on a table next to the bed, which was covered with a thick comforter decorated with flower petals. Two large pillows completed the alluring picture. They bore softer pink covers and lavender ruffles on one end.

Slocum sat down in the chair. He opened the bottle of whiskey and sniffed the aroma.

"Rotgut," he said to himself. "Pure rotgut." He put the cork back in the bottle, stretched out his legs, and waited.

Gloria appeared a few minutes later, sliding in through the door as if she were meeting a clandestine lover.

"Put my key on the table," she whispered. "Want a drink first?"

"No. First I just want to talk," he said.

"Sure. You got an hour, Joe."

She sat down in the other chair and tried to look demure. The lone lamp exaggerated her long face and ruby lips. She was trying to be coquettish, but she looked like what she was, a whore. A cheap one at that.

"Did you see Scud this afternoon?" he asked.

"Why, yes, I saw him. Why? Do you know Scud?"

"Never mind. Did he have some new women with him?"

Gloria reared back in her chair and fixed Slocum with a piercing look.

"Just what business is that of yours?" she snapped.

"I'm looking for those girls, Gloria. They were kidnapped. Two men who were taking them to Quitaque were shot and scalped by Scud and some Kiowas."

"I don't believe that for a damned minute," Gloria said.

"What, that Scud kidnapped three women or that he and his Kiowas murdered two men?"

"Any of it."

"Did he bring in three gals on horseback this afternoon?"

Gloria reached for the whiskey bottle. She pulled the cork and poured a tumbler half full. She drank half of it and her breath reeked of cheap whiskey.

"I could get killed for even talking to you," she said.

"I won't say anything to anyone about our conversation, Gloria. And I'll protect you. With my life, if necessary."

"Mister, you don't know Scud at all. He's ruthless. And he has men who will do whatever he wants. No questions asked."

"I figured as much," Slocum said. "Now just answer my question, please."

"Y-Yes," she said. She drank the rest of the whiskey in the glass. "He rode in here with three young women on horseback. The women rode bareback, and looked as if they had been in a bar fight. Their dresses were covered in dirt and torn in places. Their hair was messed up. Scud took them to Mrs. Gonzales and told her to see that they bathed and were given food, but locked in a room he keeps for such purposes."

"You mean he's done this before?"

"Sure. How do you think I wound up here? I was on a stage to Austin and next thing I knew I was in Scud's clutches.

Anita, Mrs. Gonzales, gave me a bath and I was told I could not leave. Scud told me that I was his bond servant. I believed him. That was two years ago. I've been here ever since."

"Do you know where I can find those women, Gloria?"

"I know, but I'm not going to tell you. If I do, you'll only get killed. Scud has two men outside that room with guns, and one inside with a scattergun. You wouldn't have a chance."

Before Slocum could say anything more, the door to Gloria's room burst open and Oren Scudder filled the doorway. He held a wanted flyer in his left hand and behind him stood his deputy, a double-barreled shotgun in his hands, their snouts pointed directly at Slocum.

"Gloria, get your ass out of here," Scudder barked.

For a split second time froze.

Nobody in the room moved a muscle.

Slocum heard two snicks as the deputy cocked both barrels of the Greener.

11

In moments of crisis and extreme peril, time becomes fragmented. Images are disjointed and isolated so that they are seared into the mind like acid portraits on steel. So it was when Deputy Fisk cocked the twin hammers of his double-barreled shotgun.

Several things happened at once.

The strains of "Camptown Ladies" drifted up through the floorboards as the small band struck up again after their break.

Slocum snatched up the bottle of whiskey and threw it at Sheriff Scudder. Gloria arose from her chair and screamed at the top of her voice.

Scudder ducked.

Slocum rolled out of his chair and hit the floor on his left side. At the same time, he jerked his pistol from its holster and cocked it on the rise.

Fisk squeezed both triggers and the shotgun belched fire and buckshot. He aimed where Slocum had been sitting, but Gloria stood up and caught both barrels. The heavy lead shot tore her face to shreds and mutilated it beyond recognition.

Her scream was cut off as her throat opened up and spurted a fountain of blood.

Slocum squeezed off a shot.

A black hole appeared in the center of Fisk's forehead and he dropped the shotgun, falling forward and crashing into Scudder. This threw the sheriff off balance as he clawed for his pistol.

Slocum scrambled to his feet, stepped toward Scudder.

"You draw that hogleg, Scudder," Slocum said, "and I'll put a bullet where your grub goes."

Scudder froze, his right hand turned into a rigid claw inches from his pistol.

"You bastard," Scudder snarled. "I know who you are. You're a wanted man, John Slocum."

Slocum strode toward Scudder and swiped him across the mouth with the barrel of his Colt .45. Scudder's head snapped in a half circle and blood spurted from his lips like a squashed tomato. His right hand shot to his mouth as he winced in pain.

As Scudder's knees buckled, Slocum grabbed the sheriff's pistol and jerked it from his holster

Scudder glared at Slocum, wide-eyed, as he regained his footing and stood straight up.

The flyer fell from the sheriff's hands and floated to the carpeted floor.

"You're still a wanted man, Slocum," Scudder said. "You're going to jail."

"Oh, I'm going to jail, all right, Scudder," Slocum said. "And so are you."

"Huh?" Scudder's facial muscles sagged as he tried to digest what Slocum had said to him.

"Drop that gun belt," Slocum ordered as he reached out and snatched Scudder's hat from his head.

"Hey, that's my hat," Scudder said.

Slocum sailed the hat off toward the bed. It hit the floor and skidded underneath the unused bed.

"You're lucky I don't make you shit in it, Scudder."

Scudder unbuckled his gun belt and empty holster, the knife in its sheath. He let it fall to the floor.

"This ain't goin' to get you nowhere, Slocum," the sheriff muttered.

"Oh, we're not finished yet, Scudder."

"What?"

"Take your boots off while I'm still in a good mood," Slocum said.

"You sonofabitch," Scudder said.

"Profanity will change my mood right quick," Slocum said. "Take 'em off or I'll blow 'em off."

Slocum pointed his gun barrel at Scudder's booted feet.

Scudder took off one boot, hopped around in a little circle, and removed the other one. He stood before Slocum in his socks.

"Satisfied?" Scudder snarled.

Slocum kicked the boots away with his left foot. He pointed the Colt at Scudder's midsection.

"Not quite," Slocum said. "Now unbuckle your belt and slide your pants off. Just let them fall to the floor and step toward me."

"What the hell do you think you're doin', Slocum?"

"The sight of a naked man thrills me, Scudder. When you get out of those pants, you can take off your shirt and vest, too."

"None of this is goin' to help you," Scudder said.

"No? Maybe it'll help you."

"Help me?"

"Call it a lesson in defenselessness. Like those women your worthless brother kidnapped."

"I didn't have no hand in that."

"Off with the pants and all your clothes, Scudder. I'm running out of patience."

Scudder slid his pants off and shed his vest and shirt. The badge pinned to his vest seemed to glare up at him and mock him as he stared down at it with a disconsolate look on his face.

Slocum reached down, picked up Scudder's pants, and shook them. He heard a jingle and reached into that pocket. He pulled out a set of keys and a wad of greenbacks. He stuffed them both in his right pocket.

"Now you see if your deputy has handcuffs on him," Slocum said as he dropped the pants back in a heap.

Scudder searched Fisk's back pockets and produced a set of handcuffs. He dangled them in the air.

Slocum snatched them out of Scudder's hands.

"Get his handcuff key and hand it to me," Slocum said.

Scudder dug out a tiny key from one of Fisk's front pockets and held it in the palm of his hand. Slocum moved in close, grabbed the key, and unlocked the cuffs.

"Turn around, Scudder, and put your hands behind your back."

"What the hell . . ."

"Be quick about it. This Colt's got a hair trigger and my finger's getting mighty nervous."

Scudder did as he was told and Slocum slipped the cuffs over both of his wrists.

"You stole my money, Slocum. I'll get you for that, too. And for murderin' my deputy."

"What you have, Scudder, is a handful of shit and you're about to get a lot more. Now march out of here and down the stairs."

"There are folks down there."

The band was playing "Home on the Range," and they could hear it better out in the hallway. Slocum jabbed the barrel of his pistol hard in the small of Scudder's back and the man stepped out and walked the hall to the head of the stairs.

They walked down the stairs as the band fell silent. Many

of the patrons and the other glitter gal were gathered at the bottom, all looking up at the naked man with his hands cuffed behind his back.

"Give us room," Slocum ordered, and the crowd parted. Slocum glanced at the two bartenders.

"Either one of you reach down for a gun or a bat and you'll regret it for the rest of your short life."

Both bartenders froze and raised their hands when Slocum waved his pistol in their direction.

"Out the door, Scudder," Slocum said.

As they passed the end of the bar where Horace stood, Slocum dug out some bills and laid them on the bartop.

"There's a mess up in Gloria's room," he told the barkeep. "Clean it up and this should pay for Gloria's funeral."

"Yes, sir," Horace said, but made no move to grab the money.

People stared at Scudder but remained silent until the two men parted the batwing doors and walked out into the night. Then a buzzing rose up behind the two men. They continued toward the sheriff's office.

"Where you takin' me, Slocum?" Scudder asked.

"Where you belong, Scudder. I'm taking you to jail."

"You'll pay for this, you bastard."

"Shut up, Scudder. I can always change my mind and send you straight to Boot Hill."

Scudder kept silent the rest of the way. Slocum used one of Scudder's keys to open the office. It was dark, but he saw a door past the sheriff's desk.

He pushed it open. There were two cells with iron bars. Both were empty. Both doors were open. He shoved Scudder into one of them and then closed the door. He found the right key and locked it.

"You can't do this, Slocum."

"Sleep tight," Slocum said. "I'll leave your keys on the desk."

"That won't do me no good."

"If somebody lets you out, you'd better pray that you don't meet up with me again, Scudder. I'll shoot you on sight."

"You lousy, low-down sonofabitch," Scudder snarled.

Slocum said nothing as he left, slamming the door to the cell area and locking it. He threw the keys on the desk and walked out into the night. After ejecting the empty hull, he put a fresh cartridge in the cylinder of his pistol, closed the gate, returned the gun to the holster.

Then he walked to the hotel and passed the empty desk. He climbed the stairs to Room 220 and tapped on the door.

Melissa opened it.

"Pack your bag," he said. "We're leaving."

"What? I was just getting ready for bed."

"We have to find another place to stay," he said. "I had a run-in with Sheriff Scudder. He'll tell his brother where we are."

"Where are we going to sleep?" she asked.

"Safest place I know," Slocum said.

"Where is that?"

"The livery stable," he said. "I'll grab up some pillows and bedding and off we'll go."

"Sleep in a stable? Not me."

"Suit yourself," he said. "You don't want to come, you don't have to, but when Scud comes for you, I'd appreciate it if you didn't tell him where I am."

He picked up his saddlebags, bedroll, and rifle and started for the door.

"I won't tell anyone where you are," she said.

He handed her some bills, the ones left over from Scudder's pocket.

"Here's a little money for you," he said. "See you around maybe."

"John, you don't have to do this. I don't want to be alone."

"You know where I'll be. Look for me up in the loft. If you get lonesome, that is."

She looked at the wad of money in her hand.

"Maybe this will be enough to get me back to Amarillo," she said. "Or to Quitaque."

"Melissa, I think Scud put those advertisements in the paper for you and other would-be brides. I think he knew you were coming, and from where. There is no marriage waiting for you in Quitaque or anywhere else."

"What are you going to do?" she asked, on the verge of tears.

"I'm going to see if I can find your gal friends and rescue them. If you're still here, I'll take you with me and ride back to Amarillo and see that you all get safely back home."

With that, Slocum walked out the door. He could hear Melissa sobbing as he walked down the hall.

It couldn't be helped. As soon as someone found Scudder and freed him, a bunch of guns would be after him. He wouldn't have much of a chance in a town as small as Polvo. Besides, he wanted to find those kidnapped women and Scud. Scud was a payment due in his book. He killed two men, stole four of his horses, and now it was time to pay the piper.

It was, he knew, going to be a long night.

12

Caleb Lindsey was asleep when Slocum entered the livery stable. He lay on a pile of horse blankets near the tack room at the back of the stable. When Slocum stepped on a broken piece of salt lick, the crumbling brick made a sound that woke the stable boy up.

"Who's that?" Caleb said as he sat up and rubbed his eyes.

"Wilson," Slocum said.

Caleb clambered to his feet.

Moonlight filtered in through the back doors, bathing the two men in a gauzy haze of pale white light. Slocum set his bedroll and saddlebags down next to the pile of saddle blankets.

"You awake, Caleb?" Slocum asked. "Wide awake?"

"Yes, sir. I was just dozin'. It's been pretty quiet here."

"Yesterday. Think about yesterday."

"I slept most of the day. Did some chores for my pa and ma."

"Did you notice any new horses in the stable tonight when you came to work?"

"Um, yes, sir, they was two horses come in that I never seen before."

"Did you look at their hides real close?"

"Their hides?" Caleb scratched the back of his right ear.

"Were they saddle horses, or did they have marks on them from being in harness?"

"Why, I reckon they did. I mean I noticed that right off. They weren't saddle horses, Mr. Wilson. They was wagon horses, sure as shootin'."

"And did you hear anything about three women who rode those two horses?"

"Yeah, sure. When Lew Ralston, the day man, showed me them horses, he said they was rode in here with three pretty gals on their bare backs."

"And did you think that was kind of unusual?"

"Sure I did. So did Lew. He said them gals was all mussed up, hair atangle, dirty dresses, dirty hands, and scratched legs."

"They came in with Scud, right?"

"Yep. Scud was with 'em. That's what Lew said."

"And do you know where Scud took those women?"

Caleb hesitated. He looked up at the dark ceiling and down the rows of stalls. Empty-eyed, like a lost pup.

Slocum waited. He saw that the boy was nervous and perhaps too timid to answer his question right away. Finally, Caleb met his gaze and swallowed hard.

"I guess he took 'em where he always does when some new gal comes to town," Caleb said.

"And where is that? Exactly?"

Caleb looked around furtively as if someone might overhear him. It was instinctive. He knew that they were the only two people in the stable.

"Scud, he's got him a special house. A 'dobe house where he keeps women. He has Mrs. Gonzales clean 'em up and dress 'em up, I reckon. Then he puts the gals to work at the Desert Rose or hires 'em out as cooks or laundresses."

"So Scud has done this before," Slocum said.

"Not exactly. I mean, some of the gals come to town by coach or wagon. They's been a passel of 'em come in that way the past year or so. Most work up by the mines in that big old ravine where the diggin's are. The pretty ones, they work at the saloon."

"I only saw two women at the saloon tonight."

"He had about five a month ago. Two of them run off with men, and another died."

Slocum was getting a picture of just what Scud had been up to in Polvo since he founded the town. It was an ugly picture. He drew in a deep breath and shifted his rifle from his left hand to his right.

"Tell me where that adobe house is, Caleb."

There was a twitch in Caleb's face that Slocum could see in the pale glint of moonlight that passed like a shadow between them. Caleb shifted his weight from one foot to the other.

"I don't know if I should tell you, Mr. Wilson. I mean, Scud is really my boss and he don't want people to know too much about his business. 'Specially about that 'dobe where he keeps his new gals."

"Let me put it this way, Caleb. I like you. You're a nice, decent boy. But those three women were kidnapped by Scud and he had Indian helpers who shot and killed the driver of that wagon and another boy just about your age."

"Gawley," Caleb gasped.

"Now, if I let Scud get away with that, then I'm not a man, and if you don't tell me about that adobe, you won't be much of a man either. Ever."

Slocum hammered that last word so hard it made Caleb jump.

He was ready to talk.

"You go to the end of this here street," Caleb said. "Like you was goin' out to that big ditch where they're diggin' for gold and silver. A little ways after the street runs out, there's a 'dobe off to your right. It's got a 'dobe wall around it but that ain't but about four foot high. There's a gate in front and a gate in back. I think Scud has some men with rifles walkin' inside that 'dobe wall. They can see real plain who's a-comin' and they can duck down behind it and pick off anybody who don't belong there."

"Thanks, Caleb," Slocum said. He patted the young man on the shoulder. "Now I'm going to take my bedroll and saddlebags up in the loft to get some shut-eye. I might go out later and I'll leave my rifle up there. I expect it will be there when I get back. Do we understand each other?"

"Yes, sir, I won't take your rifle."

"One more thing, Caleb."

"Yeah?"

"You don't tell anybody, and I mean anybody, that I'm bunkin' in the livery."

"Are you hidin' out, Mr. Wilson?"

Slocum smiled.

"That's right, Caleb. I'm hiding out. Now go back to your snoozin' and pay me no mind while I set up in that loft."

"I—I'm too nervous to sleep no more, Mr. Wilson. But I won't tell nobody you was here or you're bunkin' up in the hayloft."

Slocum picked up his gear and climbed a ladder into the loft. He found a spot near the front under the lone shuttered opening. He lay out his bedroll and placed his saddlebags at one end and slid his rifle under his blanket. He checked his pistol, spun the cylinder, and put it back in his holster.

He lay down, using one saddlebag for a headrest, and closed his eyes.

He would go to the adobe just before dawn when the men guarding the place would be most vulnerable, perhaps sleepy and tired and, most likely, bored. He was facing sturdy odds, he knew—at least three armed men and three defenseless women. He doubted that Scud would be there. He would find him in due time and call him to account for his vile deeds.

In moments, Slocum was asleep, but he had a timer in his head. He placed one hand on his bellygun, tucked behind his belt buckle. He wished he had not left his shotgun in Amarillo, but he had two handguns and that should be enough to return any fire he might draw from those guards. His gun belt was nearly full of .45-caliber cartridges and the bellygun held six lethal rounds of .32-caliber cartridges.

Small beams of moonlight streamed through cracks in the walls of the barn. Dust motes bobbed and floated like tiny insects, soundless as the night itself.

13

Caleb was sound asleep on the horse blankets when Slocum tiptoed from the stable some four hours later. He felt rested and refreshed and the clock in his head had worked. The moon was in another place, shining like a wan lamp over the dark shapes of the buildings and the empty streets of the town.

He kept to the shadows and walked to the end of the street, stopping every so often to listen. A gray cat streaked from between two adobe shops and scurried into deeper shadows on the other side of the street. The hunter prowling the night like a moving shadow, silent as a ghost.

Slocum saw the adobe with its wall as he reached the last building on the street. Caleb had been right. The wall afforded the guards a wide field of view. From the front at least. He wondered if one man guarded the front and the other the back. But from his perspective, the front approach would be most dangerous. In the back he saw shadowy clumps of cactus and sagebrush, other bushes, and rocks, small hillocks. He ducked into the shadows and walked back a few doors then ventured beyond the last street and started on a wide circle to come up behind the adobe.

There was no hurry. It was hours before dawn lit the sky. He took his time and stepped softly, careful to avoid crunching rocks or sand beneath his feet. It was a slow stalk, and from his vantage point on the far loop of his circle, he could only see the flat roof of the adobe. It appeared to have been constructed of wide whipsawed lumber then covered with sand and desert foliage. Not tiled, as so many were.

When he reached the apogee of his imaginary circle, Slocum crouched and approached the rear of the dwelling. As he drew closer, he crouched still lower until he was hunched close to the ground.

He stopped to reconnoiter. He stood upright very slowly and stared at the back wall. There was no guard that he could see.

But nearby, he heard a soft rustling. He crouched back down and touched the butt of his pistol. He turned in the direction of the sound and crouched low.

There were noises from the house now and he listened intently. Men were calling to one another. Cursing. Stomping around out front.

He crept toward the rustling sound and saw a depression in the earth, a shallow trench that water had scooped out during a flash flood. He walked very softly and slowly until he could look down into the depression.

He saw a splotch of white and a pair of arms. Hands covering a woman's face.

A woman lay there, curled up in a fetal position, hiding her face.

Slocum stepped closer until he was at the edge looking straight down at the frightened woman.

"D-Don't hurt me," she whimpered.

He squatted down so that she could see his face.

"I won't hurt you. I'm a friend of Melissa Warren's," Slocum whispered.

"Melissa? She's alive?"

"Yes. I found her and I was looking for you and the other two women Scud kidnapped."

"Oh, bless you, sir. I—I fear for their lives. As I fear for mine."

"You got away," he said.

"Just barely."

They spoke in whispers, but Slocum knew that sooner or later the men behind the wall would come out of their compound to look for the woman who had escaped.

"What's your name?" Slocum asked.

"Fanny. Fanny Beeson. What's yours?"

"John Slocum."

"Where's Melissa?"

"She's at the hotel. But I don't think that's a safe place for her. Can you hold out here awhile longer? I want to see if I can't get your friends away from these guards."

"I can wait," she said and her voice was close to a whimper.

"Tell me the names of the other two women, Fanny."

"Darla Whipple and Susan Lindale. But there's a man in their room with a shotgun. They're scared out of their wits."

"Maybe I can draw him out. You sit tight. I'll be back."

Slocum turned away, but did not stand up. He could hear the men in front of the adobe arguing with each other. He crept up to the back wall and waited. There was a lamp burning inside the house. Curtains masked the room itself, but there were leaks of light around the edges of the curtains. He crept along the wall and looked at the front side windows. These were dark. In the corner, he climbed over the wall, taking his time, alert to every sound.

"Well, where in hell could she be, Cal?" one of the men barked from the front of the house.

"Damn it, Rufus, I never saw her leave. Hell, maybe she's still inside. Vernon's dumber than a sack full of belly button lint."

So now Slocum knew the first names of the three men.

And the two out front were not certain that Fanny had gotten away.

"Hell, we been all through that 'dobe. She ain't there."

"Well, maybe she went into town, Cal," Rufus said.

"She must have run like a damned deer. And I didn't hear nothin' like runnin' feet since Vern yelled out she was gone."

"Then she's got to be hidin' close by somewhere," Cal said.

"Where?"

"I don't know. You say here. I'll make a big circle and see where she's hidin' out."

"I got a better idee, Cal. It's almost time for Jake and the others to relieve us. You run inside and tell Vern if he hears even one shot to open up on them two gals with both barrels."

"Damn, Cal. Scud will be mad as a hornet if'n we kill them two gals and the other'n done got away."

"Them are his orders, Rufe. He said anybody tries to come after them gals, shoot the gals."

"Yeah, Scud did say that. I'll go tell Vern if he hears a shot to blow them two gals to dust and feathers."

Slocum heard footsteps clump on the hard ground and then a secret knock on the front door. Two knocks, then two more, and finally one. He heard a latchkey jingle and then the squeak of leather hinges as the front door opened. He heard Rufus deliver the message from Cal and then a garbled voice replied. He couldn't make out the words.

The door slammed shut and the latchkey clattered again.

A few seconds later, Rufus spoke to Cal.

"He said he'd do it, Cal. He's tired of their whinin' and caterwaulin' anyways."

"Good," Cal said.

Slocum cursed under his breath. He retraced his steps and slowly climbed back over the wall. He walked hunched over back to the ditch, careful to make no noise with his boots.

Fanny was still there, cowering in the washed-out ditch. He hunkered down to whisper to her.

"Fanny," he said, "I'm taking you out of here."

"What about Darla and—"

"It's too risky. Downright dangerous. Your guard, Vernon, has orders to shoot them if he hears a gunshot from outside."

"I guess I forgot to tell you that," Fanny said.

"Three more men are coming to take over from these three. Can you get up by yourself?"

He extended his left hand. She grasped it and he pulled her out of the depression.

"Stay low and walk real quiet," he said.

He held her hand as they walked away from the adobe and did not stop until he could look back and just see the rim of the roof.

Then he headed for town. A few minutes later, he heard hoofbeats and saw the silhouettes of three men riding toward the adobe.

It had been a close call.

If he had shot either of those two outside guards, those other two women would be dead now, torn to pieces by buckshot.

He looked down at Fanny and wondered.

Were those other two women as stupid as she?

14

It was obvious to Slocum that Fanny had gotten the beauty treatment from Anita Gonzales. Once he got a good look at her in the moonlight, he could see that her hair had been washed and combed. She smelled of perfume and scented powder. She was feminine and petite with an ample bust and full, voluptuous lips, which glistened in the moonlight like ruby cherries.

When he guided her to the stable's back door, she looked up at the barn in surprise.

"Where are you taking me?" she asked.

"I can't take you to the hotel. Scud would find you there."

"But isn't that where Melissa is?"

"Yes, for now, but I'm worried about her, too."

"Why?"

"It's a long story," he said. He opened the door as quietly as possible and held a finger to his lips so that Fanny would know to be silent.

The horses in the stalls nickered softly. The musty smell of hay and horse apples permeated the air inside the stable. Moonbeams slashed the dark with gleaming lances, and dust motes glittered in the soft light like ghostly moths.

Caleb was now lying on his stomach atop the saddle blankets and rattling a light snore through his nostrils. The two stepped lightly past him and Slocum pointed Fanny toward the ladder. She looked up at him with raised eyebrows, but she climbed the ladder. Slocum followed her. At the top he led her to where he had placed his bedroll. He pointed to it, then pulled his rifle out from underneath.

"Lie down," he said.

Fanny raised a hand to her breast as if to show shame. He smiled at her. The thin shafts of moonlight sprayed across her face, and he could not be certain if she was wary of him or afraid.

"Down there?" she whispered.

"It's my bedroll. It won't bite you."

Fanny chuckled softly.

"I'm wondering about you, John. Do you bite?"

"Only if bitten," he said and helped her sit down atop his bedroll. She patted it and he squatted next to her, disturbing the straw under his boots. She touched one of the saddlebags and pressed down on it as if testing its softness.

"Is this supposed to be your pillow?" she asked.

"Call it a headrest," he said.

"It's soft, but lumpy."

"If you hear a clink, that's a bottle of Kentucky bourbon. Snakebite medicine."

"Oh," she cooed, "I haven't tasted bourbon since I left Missouri."

Slocum reached over and fumbled in his saddlebag for the bottle of bourbon. He pulled it out, uncorked it. The bottle was almost full.

"Have a taste," he said.

"Thanks, I need it after what I've been through."

She sipped from the bottle and handed it to Slocum. He took a swallow and handed the bottle back.

Fanny shook her head.

"That was enough for now. Helps to calm my nerves."

"Tell me about Scud," Slocum said. "What did he say he was going to do with you and the other women?"

"At first, he didn't say much. He mainly spoke to those Injuns that rode with us. Then they left and he brought us to that horrid place where you found me."

"And was Mrs. Gonzales there waiting for you?"

"No, she came out later. Scud told us that we were going to work for him at his saloon. That we had to look pretty and he would furnish us nice clothes and see that we were bathed and our hair washed and combed. He made a lot of promises."

"Did you protest? I mean, did you question him about taking you against your will?"

"Why, yes, we all put up a fuss, but he said that we were his bond servants and had better get used to it."

"Then what happened?" Slocum asked.

"Darla got real mad and wanted him to let us all loose. Scud told us all that we could not leave and that if we tried, he would shoot us dead."

"Just like that," Slocum said.

"Just like that. He meant it, too. That man makes my skin crawl. He's mean and heartless."

"You know he killed the men on that wagon."

"I knew he or one of them Injuns killed Ruddy, our driver. I don't know what happened to Jeremy."

"He died shortly after you were taken."

"Oh no," she said. "Darla was sweet on him, I think. Such a nice young man."

Slocum started to put the bottle of whiskey back in his saddlebag, but Fanny touched his hand.

"Not yet," she said. "I think I need another drink. I can't get over Jeremy being killed."

"Help yourself," he said, and uncorked the bottle, handed it to her. This time, Fanny took a swallow, then another right away. She handed the bottle back to him and extended both arms, shook them like a bird ruffling its feathers.

"Oooh, that did the trick," she said.

Slocum corked the bottle and left it out of the bag, placing in on a nest of straw where it could be easily reached by either of them.

"You better get some sleep," he said. "No telling what we'll face in the morning. I've got to get Melissa out of that hotel and I expect Scud will be hunting me."

"From what I've seen, this isn't much of a town. Scud said there was only one hotel and a boardinghouse where we would all stay and that we had no chance of ever escaping."

"Did you know his brother is the sheriff?"

Fanny shook her head.

"No. He just said we could expect no help from the law. We belonged to him. Period."

Slocum said nothing. He let her words sink in so that he was completing the picture of Scud he had been building in his mind. The man was ruthless and cruel. He obviously saw women as chattel, as commodities in his scheme to acquire wealth, no matter the cost. He had seen such men before, and knew how hungry they were for power. Such men did not care how they got that power, but the more they got, the more they wanted.

Fanny looked around. She sniffed the air and closed her eyes for a moment. Slocum watched her, wondered what she was thinking.

"Oh, yes," she whispered.

"Huh?"

"The smells in here remind me of home," she said.

"Home?"

"A barn like this. We had one. Not quite as big, but we hayed every summer and filled the loft with hay for the winter. We had cattle and horses. I spent many hours playing in our little barn just outside of Springfield, back in Missouri. The smells remind me of my childhood and that barn. It's full of memories."

"Good ones, I hope," Slocum said when she paused and closed her eyes again, sniffed deeply of the scents in the stable.

"Mostly good," she said. "My brother and I thought of the barn as our sanctuary, a place where we could do things that our folks would never know about. I had some of my dolls up there in that loft, and Kenny, my big brother, kept his toy soldiers and his slingshot up there." She laughed. "He unloaded our pa's shot shells and used the lead balls in his slingshot to shoot the rats that scurried in the rafters."

She looked long and wistful at him. Slocum said nothing, trying to picture Fanny as a little girl, playing with her dolls up in the hayloft.

"I lost my cherry up in that barn," Fanny said, so matter-of-factly that her words caught Slocum by surprise.

"You . . ."

"Lost my cherry, my maidenhead, my virginity. Haven't you ever heard that term before?"

"Yes, but seldom from a woman," he said.

Fanny laughed low in her throat.

"I said we had fun, John. Lots of fun."

"You had a boyfriend?"

"Well, not then. Not when I lost my cherry."

Slocum swallowed hard, unable to speak, to ask the question swirling around in his mind like a top.

"Who . . . who took your . . ."

"My cherry? Kenny did. My big brother. We were just talking and the talk got around to the difference between boys and girls. He said he would show me his if I showed him mine, so we did that. I took off my panties and he took off his pants and his undershorts and I saw his thing. I was amazed."

"You had never seen one before?" Slocum asked, his voice growing husky.

"Oh, I had caught glimpses of Pa's and Ken's, but they just looked like lumps of flesh to me. Ken's thing was growing while he looked at my privates. He asked me to spread my legs so that he could see more of my little pie. It didn't have much hair on it then, and while he looked, his pecker just grew hard and stiff and stood straight up."

"What did you do then?" Slocum asked. He was becoming aroused himself. The way she talked, so frankly, with a certain air of wonderment and innocence, and one of her hands was in her lap, the fingers stroking a spot between her legs.

"I asked Kenny if I could touch it, and he said yes if he could touch my little honey pie. So, I reached over and stroked his pecker at first and then he asked me to put my hand around it. I did that and I could feel the blood. I could feel it pulse as if I was holding his heart. And he touched me between my legs and then he slid a finger in there and I thought I was going to die right then."

Slocum gulped, caught up in the story and so aroused his pants bulged at his crotch.

"And then what happened?" he rasped.

"He started pushing his finger in and out of me and I gushed all over his finger. He touched something inside my honey pot that was like a hot shock of electricity, like when you rub your hands on a rug and then touch a piece of metal. I jumped and squeezed him, and then, then it just happened."

"What happened?"

"Kenny said he wanted to stick his pecker in me, and I took off my dress. He took off his clothes and we played with each other for a minute or two and then he crawled on top of me and dipped down. The next thing I knew, his pecker was inside me and I was almost crying out loud with the thrill of it, the pleasure. He went in and out and I felt my insides explode and get hot and all runny with water or something. There was a little sting when he broke my cherry but it didn't hurt all that much, and then he said he was coming and he did, inside me. I could feel it and I was so happy I pulled his head down and kissed him."

"Yeah," Slocum said, his voice dreamy and low.

"We did it a lot after that, and he sometimes brought a friend up to the loft, a boy friend, and he would tell his friend that he could do it to me. Kenny watched. And sometimes both Kenny and his friend fucked me, first one and then the other."

"That was quite an experience," Slocum said.

"I enjoyed it, but that's why I left home. My brother wouldn't leave me alone and then at church I learned how wrong it was, brother and sister, so I ran away. Kenny was very possessive. He was jealous of any boys I liked at school."

"How do you feel about it now?"

She looked at him and moonlight glinted in her eyes, like a wispy vapor of smoke. She leaned closed to him and rubbed his crotch.

"It's been a long time," she said. "And nothing I've had since has been as good as those times with my brother."

"I'm not your brother," he said, starting to draw away.

"No, but I want you, John. Up here. I want you real bad. Do you want me?"

He heaved a deep sigh.

"Lord, yes," he said and touched her breasts, felt the nubbins of her nipples harden like tiny acorns.

"Take me, then," she said.

He reached between her legs and touched her panties. They were wet, soaked with the fluids from her pussy, and her hand was unbuckling his gun belt and the other was stroking his manhood so that his pants stretched to the breaking point between his legs.

Frantically, they both undressed and came together in a lusty embrace. He kissed her and felt her heat flow through him like warm wine. Then she lay down on her back and he rose above her like a conquering warrior, fully ready to drink from her loving cup.

15

Fanny was as frisky as a spring lamb. Slocum dipped his wick into her and she became animated, lifting her legs high in the air and rocking beneath him like a rowboat anchored in a storm. He plumbed her depths, and her body jolted as if hit by a thunderbolt. She cried out softly and gently scratched his back with her fingernails.

Her brown hair was silky, soft to his touch. Her body was lithe and pliant, and as they made love, she mewed like a kitten in his ear. When she was in the throes of her first jolting orgasm, she quivered all over and her mouth opened, her eyelashes flapping as she opened and closed her eyes.

"So good," she murmured. "Don't stop."

"No," he said. "There's more to come."

"Yes, yes," she breathed, and he increased the speed of his strokes. Her loins answered the thrusts and she rose and fell beneath him like an ocean comber in a storm.

Slocum held his seed through sheer willpower, and Fanny kept urging him on, kept calling to him that she wanted him to explode inside her.

"You're amazing," she said. "Can we do it doggie fashion?"

"Sure," Slocum said.

She turned over after he uncoupled and got up on her hands and knees so that he could enter her from the rear. He pushed inside her, past the soft folds of her portal, and Fanny bucked against him, overcome with a rush of pleasure. He pumped back and forth, delving deep into her vulva, grasping her legs with both hands and pulling her toward him as he pushed.

"Oh, John," she said, "that's so good, I just keep coming and coming."

"I can't last much longer, Fanny," he gruffed. "I feel it coming. It's boiling and . . ."

She pushed back hard and Slocum drove deep to the mouth of her womb. He shuddered as his seed exploded and spurted like milk into her chamber. It was as if rockets had shot skyward in his brain. She screamed softly and reached back to touch him as her body spasmed with twin orgasms that set her entire body to tingling as if she had been plunged in an icy stream then stuffed into a roaring furnace. She shivered and shook as he pulled out of her, sated and exhausted but suffused with a pleasure beyond description.

They lay together on their backs, she on the bedroll, Slocum next to her on a bed of scratchy straw. No matter. He was content.

So was Fanny.

They floated there in their matching euphorias without speaking. She clasped his hand in hers, and when he looked over after a few minutes, he saw that she was fast asleep.

Slocum moved her hand slowly back to rest on her naked tummy, then got up and dressed. He buckled his gun belt after he pulled on his boots and tiptoed across the loft and descended the ladder.

A voice from the darkness startled him.

"Mr. Wilson, they's somebody here to see you. He just

come in and I was about to call up there to see if you was awake." It was Caleb Lindsey speaking. Wide awake and fidgety as a kid called to the front of the schoolroom.

"Who is it?" Slocum asked.

"It's one of the Messicans from the diggin's," Caleb whispered. "He's just outside. Come lookin' for you."

"Did he say why?" Slocum asked.

"Nope, he just said it was *muy importante*. Real important, he means."

"I know what it means," Slocum said. "Where is he?"

"Out back. Like he don't want nobody to know he's here."

"Do you know him, Caleb?"

"I knowed him when he first come here. We don't see any of them Messicans 'cept when they come to town once't a month or so. Scud, he keeps 'em out at the diggin's pretty much."

"I don't get it," Slocum said. "Something wrong with Mexicans being in town?"

"I dunno," Caleb said. He looked down at his feet as if he was ashamed of something, or didn't want to talk about the way Mexicans were treated in Polvo.

"All right, I'll talk to him. One thing you ought to know, Caleb."

"Yeah? What's that?"

"There's a woman up in the loft. Sleeping. I rescued her from Scud. Another secret I'm going to ask you to keep."

"Why sure, Mr. Wilson, I won't tell nobody."

"Not even your folks. I mean it."

"No, sir, not nobody."

"Fine," Slocum said and walked to the rear of the stable. He walked through the small door where he and Fanny had entered earlier and looked around for the Mexican.

"Mr. Wilson?"

Slocum saw a shadowy figure standing near the water trough next to the side rail fence.

"I'm Wilson. Who are you?"

The man approached Slocum. He took off his hat and gripped it with both hands as if he had just entered a church.

"I am José Delgado," the man said. "I was at the saloon tonight when you made Sheriff Scudder walk down the stairs with no clothes on."

"And?"

"I thought it was very brave. You are a brave man, Mr. Wilson."

"Scudder was responsible for shooting a woman dead up in her room. His deputy pulled the trigger, but Scudder brought him there to get after me."

"There was much talk after you left. Someone showed us the flyer with your face on it. There is a two-thousand-dollar reward for your capture."

"So did you come here to collect the reward, José?"

Slocum let his hand drop to the butt of his Colt. Just in case.

"Oh, no, I come to ask you to help us. For I know you are a brave man. Sheriff Scudder, he is a bad man. A very bad man and nobody ever stood up to him like you did."

"You speak very good English, José."

"I had schooling, Mr. Wilson, and I practiced my English since I was a boy. A little boy."

"What kind of help are you asking for?"

"I have a story to tell you, and then I wish that you would ride with me to the mines so that I can show you how we live and why we hate Scud and his brother. We are prisoners and we are treated like dogs."

"Can't you get away?" Slocum asked.

"Those of us who tried have the lilies over their graves," José said.

"You mean . . ."

"I mean that if you run away, Scud's men will hunt you down and shoot you. In front of everybody. Some they killed with the rope."

"Hanged some of your people?"

"Many," Delgado said. "This is what I want you to see. How we live. Where we live."

"What good will that do?" Slocum asked.

"Maybe you will want to help us fight these men. What they are doing is making slaves of my people. Even the whites here in Polvo are afraid of Scud and his brother, the sheriff."

"Do you have a horse?" Slocum asked.

José pointed beyond the fence.

"I have a mule," he said.

"I'll saddle up and meet you where your mule is tied."

José put his straw hat back on his head.

Before he turned and left, Slocum looked hard at José and asked a question.

"Are you allowed to come to town?" he asked.

"Ah, some of us can come once a month and we must be back to work by morning. I do not have much time left, but I wanted to see you and talk to you."

"I won't be long, José."

Slocum went back into the stables. Caleb was standing there with Ferro all saddled.

"I knew you was a-goin' to the diggin's with that Messican, Mr. Wilson. So I got your horse all ready."

"How did you know that, Caleb?"

"Because I heard from José what you done with Sheriff Scudder. Boy oh boy, there's goin' to be hell to pay, I reckon."

"You reckon right, Caleb. I think I made an enemy when I locked Sheriff Scudder up in the hoosegow."

"José said you marched him out of the saloon buck naked."

"Well, Scudder was buck naked. I wasn't."

"That's what I mean."

"Remember our secrets, Caleb."

"Not a word, Mr. Wilson, only . . ."

"Only what?"

"Only José says that ain't your real name. He said you was a wanted man. Back in Georgia."

"That's right. I'm not guilty, but some people want to stretch my neck back home."

"Do I keep callin' you Mr. Wilson?"

"No, Caleb, the cat's out of the bag now. You can call me by my real name. It's John Slocum."

"Okay."

Slocum took the reins and led Ferro out of the barn.

"You take care, Mr. Slocum," Caleb said as Slocum walked his horse through the open big door.

José opened the corral gate and closed it behind Slocum. He climbed onto his mule as Slocum hiked up into the saddle atop Ferro.

"Lead the way, José," Slocum said.

"It is not far, but we will go a different way because there might be men looking for you."

"Is Scudder out of jail, then?"

"Yes. Some men from the saloon went to the jail with his clothes and found him."

"That's too bad. Maybe I should have thrown away the keys."

José laughed and they rode between buildings and out onto the rocky land beyond the town. There was no road, no trail, just an empty pewtered desert with its dark shapes of cactus and sage, jackrabbits and slinking coyotes, the distant call of an owl. It was still dark, but the moon was drifting above the horizon through wisps of clouds that were high and thin in the dark starred sky, like streamers of smoke floating from some long-ago campfire.

Soon they began to see the murky shapes of adobe dwellings. These seemed to have no pattern, but were in small bunches, homely and humble as deserted beehives.

"This is where we all live," José said. "We must be

careful. There are men guarding this place. They ride horses and they have rifles."

"Where are we going?" Slocum asked.

"I will take you to my house. Then we will ride to the place where we dig in the mines for gold and silver."

"Are you paid for this work?"

José cackled a dry laugh.

"A little bit of money, each month. Scud gives us rice and beans, and we hunt for rabbits and the coyote. We starve and we do not have much money."

Slocum swore under his breath.

They rode up to a small *jacal* with a rickety fence and a small adobe. There was a fire pit outside. José dismounted and tied his mule to the back fence. Slocum slid out of the saddle. The gate was held shut with baling wire. José opened it and the two men walked to the hut. José tapped on the door. It opened.

A small woman wearing a shabby dress and worn sandals opened the door. She bade them enter and Slocum had to duck through the small doorway.

A lamp burned low on a table in the single room. They passed the table and Slocum saw people sitting against the walls. There was no furniture besides the small table.

"This is where we all live," José said. "This is my wife, Perla, and those are her folks on one side of the room, my folks on the other. We have two little children. They are asleep in the corner."

"All of you live in this one room?"

"It is a dungeon," Perla said. She was young and pretty, but she had old eyes, puffy flesh beneath them, and the scrubbed hands of an old washerwoman.

"Does everyone here in this little village live this way?" Slocum asked.

"Como animales," José's mother said as she stood up, bracing herself against her husband's knees as she rose. "Like animals."

"Mama Delgado," José said.

"Can you buy food?" Slocum asked. "If you have money, I mean."

"We can buy sugar and salt, but most of the time we do not have enough even for that."

Slocum reached into his pocket and pulled out some bills. He put them on the table.

"Now do you want to see where we dig?" José asked.

Slocum was standing slightly stooped. The room was small, the ceiling low. He had a strong feeling of claustrophobia, of being not in a home, but in a jail cell. He wanted to leave before he choked up at the sight of so many people living together in such a small place. They were not living there, they were confined there, by a cruel and heartless man, or a bunch of such men.

He thought of an old saying he had heard back in Georgia, from his father.

"Whatever poor people do," William Slocum had said, "is against the law."

These people were poor. They were not lawbreakers. But they were treated like criminals.

"Yes, let's go, José. I want to see all that you're up against."

"You will see," he said, "but you will never really know. We are the only ones who know."

Slocum's jaw hardened as he followed José out of the hovel where he and his family lived.

He had already seen too much.

And he knew that he still did not know what they were going through.

A light breeze sprang up as the two men rode out from the *barrio* and the moon was setting. It was cool, but the clouds had all disappeared and the dawn sun would rise and bake the harsh land as if to bring the earth a taste of hell.

16

The diggings, Slocum thought, were along a deep wide gulley that was a miniature of Palo Duro Canyon. There were holes in the walls and timbers lying stacked next to tarped-over boxes of dynamite, fuses, caps, shovels, pickaxes, and other tools, hammers and iron wedges for splitting logs, and ropes and pry bars.

"It is quiet now," José said. "But when the sun comes up, there will be many men digging in those caves and setting dynamite. You do not see the ore carts because they are in the mines, but there will be wagons and men breaking rocks we bring out, with sledgehammers and dull axes."

"I see some wheelbarrows, too. A lot of them."

"That is what I do. Men fill the wheelbarrows with rocks and I haul them over there where other men break up the rocks and load the rocks into wagons."

"Where do they take the ore when the wagons are filled?" Slocum asked.

"They bring teams in and haul the ore to a smelter in Amarillo. We do not know what happens to the gold and silver after that because we do not get any of it."

"You're paid in greenbacks?"

José looked wildly up at Slocum. "We get paid mostly in chits, but we get some greenbacks and some coins."

"I'd like to see one of those chits," Slocum said.

"They are only good at the saloon or the small store where we buy salt, flour, and coffee. And we pay the high prices, whether we use the chits, the greenbacks, or the coins."

José reached into one of his pockets and pulled out a piece of paper. He handed it to Slocum.

"That is a chit," José said.

Slocum looked it over. It was printed and bore the legend SCUDDER MINING COMPANY. The rest of it looked similar to a bank check and spelled out the amount of money the chit was worth. In this case it was fifty cents.

"Four bits," Slocum said as he handed the chit back to José.

"We could wipe our asses with these chits," José said. "Sometimes I am much tempted."

They rode down the length of the deep and wide ravine, a ravine that was scarred by diggings, holes blasted in the walls, and wheel tracks lacing the terrain around them. There were lots of horse and mule tracks, as well.

"This is where we work," José said. "Every day, even on Sunday."

"You have no church?"

José shook his head.

"We pray, some of us, but it is a secret."

"Do the old folks in your house work?"

"Yes. They clean the latrines and cook the food for all of us who work in the diggings. They work very hard."

The dark sky was slowly paling, the stars turning dim. The moon was losing its bright radiance. José looked at the sky.

"Time for you to go, Mr. Slocum. I must get my gloves and work boots."

"Before I go, José, tell me—are there any men like you

here who will fight alongside me? Who will shoot to kill if they have to?"

"There are such men, yes, but we have no guns. We do not even have machetes."

"If I brought you guns, would you and other men be able to load and shoot them?"

"Yes. I myself am a good shot, and I know several others. Some hunted buffalo before the war and some killed the antelope and the deer. But we have no guns."

"How many men here will back me if I go up against Scud and his brother?"

"Many," José said. "At least one dozen. Maybe more. I will find out."

"I'll be seeing you, José," Slocum said, and rode away.

"Go with God," José said. "Come back with guns."

17

On his way back to town, on the other side of the barrio, Slocum encountered a man on horseback. The man was carrying a rifle. He hailed Slocum with a wave of his arms, and Slocum reined up Ferro.

"Hold on there," the man said.

"I'm holding on."

"State your business," the man said when he rode up close and halted his horse.

He was about thirty years old, Slocum figured, but his face had been ravaged by smallpox and was deeply pitted. He wore a small felt hat, and a bandanna around his neck that had faded from blue to a pale pink from many washings. His pistol was a converted Colt Navy, and only a few bullets were on his gun belt. He was thin, almost emaciated, and looked as if he might blow away in a strong wind if he didn't have a couple of bricks in his pocket.

"I'm just out for a morning ride," Slocum said.

"You got no business 'round these diggings," the man said.

"What diggings?" Slocum said.

"I see you comin' from that ravine yonder. Hell, you couldn't miss it."

"Well, I did."

"What're you doin' around Polvo?"

"I lost some horses. I'm looking for them."

The man snorted in disbelief.

"Likely you come to the wrong place, mister. Ain't no stray horses 'round here."

"My mistake," Slocum said.

"I ought to run you in," the skinny man said.

"For what?"

"Trespassin', that's what."

Slocum dropped his attitude of amiability. He narrowed his eyes and hardened his jaw.

"Far as I know," Slocum said, "this is open range out here, and I'm just riding through it, looking for my lost horses."

The thin man reared back as if caught off guard. Which he was.

"It ain't open range. You see all them adobes back yonder? They's a town there. And this land is owned by somebody."

"Who? Scud?"

The man reacted as if Slocum had slapped him in the face. He stood up in the stirrups and started to lower his rifle.

"You know Scud?"

"Never met him," Slocum replied.

"Well, he owns all this land and he ain't no man to dally with."

"Fine. I'm trespassing. What are you going to do about it?" Slocum paused, then continued, "If you level that Spenser at me, it'll be the last thing you do on this earth."

The rifle stopped moving.

"You push pretty hard for a man what's breakin' the law, mister."

"Turn your horse and ride back where you came from," Slocum ordered.

The man's jaw dropped at this insolence, this haughtiness, the brazen act of defiance.

"And if'n I don't?"

"That horse you're on is going to have an empty saddle," Slocum said.

"You threatenin' me, ain't you?"

"Could be I am. Could also be that I'm warning you. You want to keep breathing, don't you?"

The man thought it over for several seconds. He lifted his rifle to its former upright position, resting the butt on his right leg.

"Well, you just skedaddle on outta here, mister, before I change my mind. We got us a right smart jail in Polvo and a sheriff that's mean as a butcher shop dog."

"I'll be on my way," Slocum said, switching to his amiable tone. "Mighty nice to meet somebody who knows the lay of the land."

Slocum touched his index finger of his left hand to the brim of his hat and turned Ferro away from the rider. He banked on the man not shooting him in the back, but he was ready to hunch over the saddle horn, turn, and draw his pistol if he heard a rustle from the Spencer carbine the man carried.

After he had ridden a hundred yards or so, he turned slowly in the saddle to look back at the guard he had encountered. The man was riding away, back toward the barrio. Slocum looked beyond at the paling sky, the fading stars, and the wan lusterless moon. It would be daybreak in a matter of minutes.

Slocum rode down a side street, then turned toward the hotel. He tied Ferro across the street at a hitch ring in front of a small dry goods store and walked across the street to the Excelsior. There was a lamp burning in the lobby, and another behind the check-in counter. A burly man stood where Parsons had been the night before. He wore a porkpie hat and a string tie that was bright red. His shirt was blue with black stripes, and his trousers were well-worn. He was tall with a thick bulbous nose and folds of fat around his neck.

"You checking in?" the man asked.

"Nope. I have a room."

"Then I bid you good mornin'," the man said with just a trace of an Irish brogue in his voice. Slocum nodded and proceeded to the stairs.

He walked down the hall to Room 220 and tapped softly on the door.

No answer.

He knocked again. Slightly louder this time and waited.

He pressed his ear against the door and listened for any sounds of stirring within the room.

He turned the doorknob, but the room was locked.

He knocked again, loudly this time. Rap, rap, rap, rap.

Still no one came to open the door.

He shook the doorknob. And listened.

Finally, he walked away and back down the stairs. He went to the counter and the man looked up from his desk.

"Checking out?" the man said.

"No. I need my key. Room 220."

The man stood up. But he did not look at the keys on the board.

"Lady checked out about an hour ago. Are you Mr. Wilson?"

"I am."

"Sheriff Scudder said you wouldn't be needin' that room no more, so I signed you out."

"So the sheriff took Miss Warren with him? Was he alone?"

"Yep."

"Was Miss Warren his prisoner?"

"Didn't look like it. She had a carpetbag with her and I

gathered she was here to work at the saloon. Pretty gal like that."

"Do you know where Scudder took her?"

"Nope. Don't know and don't care. You aim to stay another night, you got to sign the register."

"I'll let you know," Slocum said. "The saloon open this time of day?"

The man behind the counter looked out at the brightening street.

"Nope. Too early. It don't open until nigh noon. You want something to eat, there's a little café a block or so away, past the Desert Rose. That's where all the drunks go when the saloon closes. And I'd say it's been closed a good hour or so judging by the sun out there on the street. My name's Phil Dunegan, and I'll be on duty here 'till dark. Plenty of rooms left."

"I'll bet," Slocum said.

He walked out of the hotel and over to where Ferro was tied. He stood there for a few minutes. Hunger gnawed at his stomach, but he didn't savor the idea of eating at a public place, even this early.

He looked at a post nearby and saw a piece of paper fluttering in the morning breeze.

He walked over and looked at the flyer.

There was a drawing of him that was a replica of the ones he had seen before. But it showed him as he was now, with a stippled chin and black hat, black shirt.

WANTED, the dodger stated. And underneath: *For murder*. Then below that: *Dead or Alive*.

At the very bottom, there was this announcement in large block letters: $2000.00 REWARD.

"You didn't waste any time, did you, Scudder?" Slocum muttered.

Then he untied his reins, mounted Ferro, and rode toward the stables.

And the livery was right behind the sheriff's office.

Good, he thought. I can kill two birds with one good chunk.

Morning seeped through the town, scrubbing up all the deep shadows and thinning them out like castoff garments of vanished people.

If Sheriff Scudder was in, Slocum vowed, he was going to kill him.

First, though, he would stuff that wanted dodger down his throat.

The anger boiled in him like the sun rising over the eastern horizon, raw and raging like a fire released from the bowels of hell.

18

The sheriff's office was dark inside when Slocum rode up to the hitch rail and reined in Ferro. He waited there for a few minutes, looked up and down the deserted street. A few doors beyond, and across the street, he saw lamps burning and a sign outside that read ROSITA'S CAFÉ. He could see shadowy figures sitting at tables near the front window and steamed edges on the upper part of the glass.

His stomach churned and growled.

Those damned flyers were posted on every building, every stanchion, every storefront. The ink was still wet on most of them. There was probably a printer in town, and Scudder had made him turn out those dodgers at a pretty fair clip and hired some kid to nail them up. Well, Slocum thought, that was one way to handle anger, and he wondered if Scudder had upped the reward money from $1,000 to $2,000, or if Georgia thought he was worth more after all these years.

The café was too close to the jail to suit Slocum. Even a town this small must have more than one or two places where a man could buy hot grub. He tied his horse at a hitch rail at the end of the street and walked to another street in the next block. Each street was only about three blocks long, he figured, four at the most. He carried his rifle with him, just in case someone might be tempted to steal it.

Most of the stores along Second Street were closed, but he was following his nose now and looking for a specific business that had nothing to do with food, except in a roundabout way. He passed little huts with signs that proclaimed that the owners did sewing or sold pottery. There was a harness maker near the stables on the same street nearly opposite the livery. There was even a silversmith and an apothecary with all kinds of bottles and tins of salve in its window. At the very end of the street, he found one of the places he was seeking. The board storefront had one window and one door. The sign read: TIM CHANDLER, GUNSMITH. OPEN 8:00 A.M. CLOSE AT DARK. He figured he would have about an hour to wait before the store opened.

He kept walking, following his nose. He sniffed the air, turned a corner, and saw a little building where smoke was rising from a chimney. It was a homely adobe, and the aroma of meat and corn tortillas wafted to him on the morning air. There was no window, but a sign leaning against the building told him what was inside: *Carne asada. Juevos rancheros. Bistec. Puerco, pollo y mas. Cerveza, café, y agua fresco.* His stomach twisted into a knot and he went inside the café, which was twice as long as it was wide.

The oak door swung open on leather hinges. As soon as he entered, Slocum knew that he was in another world. There was a counter on the left, with handmade wooden stools. Round, rough-hewn tables were scattered in the center, with square tables, the larger ones, against the right wall. Some of these were separated by whipsawed boards acting as privacy partitions.

Mexicans sat on the stools and at some of the tables. All of them looked at him when he stood there in the natural light. Beyond the counter, he saw open windows with shelves where food from the kitchen could be placed. Two young girls wearing dainty aprons carried food and drinks to the tables, and a man and woman, both with graying hair and heavily lined faces, served the men sitting on the stools. They both wore handmade aprons and white garments that appeared to have been starched and pressed.

Slocum walked to a table, sat down, and took off his hat. He heard the whispers all around him. The single word that stood out was *gringo*. He looked around at the decorated walls. Colored tiles ran midway up the long wall where the square tables stood, and there were little shelves attached to the adobe with heavy dowels on which statues of religious figures were arranged. These were made of clay, fired in a kiln, and painted with bright colors. There were also crude paintings on the wall, one of a young bullfighter caping a roaring black bull and another of a young woman wearing a black mantilla, with large brown eyes and mahogany skin. Alongside the paintings were little miniature mosaics of dogs and cats, and a tintype of an old Mexican town, drab and tawny, with a church steeple rising above the humble rooftops.

One of the young waitresses walked over to Slocum's table. She looked at him with liquid eyes, her twin braids dangling over both shoulders, each tied with bright green, yellow, and white ribbons. She wore small silver earrings inset with polished jade stones.

Slocum looked up at her and said in perfect Spanish: *"Parece que estoy in Mejico."*

The girl blushed and laughed shyly.

"You are in a part of Mexico," she said in English with a faint Spanish accent. "What once was Mexico." Murmurs arose around them, commenting on the girl's statement.

"Me muero de hambre," Slocum said.

"You are dying of hunger," she replied, and handed him a slate. The menu was written in Spanish and Slocum ordered eggs, bacon, and beef steak with beans, speaking in the Spanish tongue.

"You understand Spanish," he said to the girl, "but do you speak it? I have heard only English pass your lips."

"*Yo hablo la langua de mis padres, pero yo hablo Ingles, tambien.*"

Slocum laughed and she laughed with him.

"I will bring your order," she said. The old man behind the counter opened a small door and walked over to Slocum's table. He brought an empty cup and a pot of steaming coffee. Without asking, he set the cup down in front of Slocum and poured hot coffee clear to the brim.

"You are a stranger here in Polvo," the man said.

"Yes."

"I am Jorge Alessandro, the owner of this place. I saw your picture in many places this morning when I came to open up."

"And you're thinking about the two-thousand-dollar reward for my capture," Slocum said evenly.

"No, I do not think that," Jorge said. "Because I was in the *cantina* last night when you marched the sheriff down the stairs and out the door. I thought you were a very brave man and I admire a brave man."

"You could probably be arrested for saying such things out loud, Jorge."

"Why do you come here to Polvo? It is not a town one visits or even passes through on his way to somewhere else."

"I came here because of four women. Three were kidnapped by Scud, and I found one near an overturned wagon with two dead men in it. Scud was with a small band of Kiowa, who scalped the two dead men and stole four horses I was taking to the Goodnight ranch."

"I see," Jorge said. He nodded at the coffee cup and Slocum picked it up, blew on it, and took a sip.

"Very good coffee," he said.

"It is the way we roast the beans, Mr. Slocum."

"Best coffee in Texas," Slocum said. "Bar none."

"And the best in Mexico, as well."

The two men laughed and Slocum lifted a hand and extended it. The two shook hands.

"Now you are a hunted man," Alessandro said.

"I am a hunted man hunting other men. I found one of the girls hiding in a ditch behind an adobe where the two other kidnapped women are being held against their will. And the one I brought here to Polvo was taken from the hotel by Sheriff Scudder."

"As I said, you are a brave man, but you fight against great odds, dangerous men. Scudder and those who work for his brother will shoot you on sight. The wanted paper says 'dead or alive.' I think Scudder would prefer you dead after you humiliated him in front of so many people."

The young waitress brought a tray with his food on it and set down the plates, silverware, and a large checkered napkin.

"Is there anything else you wish?" she asked.

"No, thank you," Slocum said.

"That is my daughter, Esperanza," Jorge said. "We are allowed to work here in town because I pay Scud a large percentage of what we earn."

"Why did you come here?"

"I have two sons who were, how do you say it, attracted here by an advertisement in a San Antonio newspaper. They thought they were going to work on a cattle ranch, but one of my sons smuggled a letter out, which was mailed to me, and I learned that both sons were prisoners, forced to work in the mines and paid little or no money."

"Still, you came here and were not taken to the mines like all the others. I was out there this morning with a man named José Delgado. He showed me where he lived and I saw the diggings."

Jorge crouched over the table in an intimate exchange.

"Then you know, Mr. Slocum," he said.

"I know. And I want to help those people. Your sons, if they are still there."

"They are still there. How will you help them?"

"José said he could give me a dozen men who can shoot and who are not afraid. I am going to try and get them rifles and pistols so that they can rebel against this injustice that has been dealt them."

"You are not only a brave man," Jorge said, "you are a crazy man."

He leaned back in his chair and did not speak until Slocum had finished his meal.

"Smoke?" Slocum said, and fished two cheroots out of his shirt pocket. He handed one to Jorge.

"Yes, I will smoke one of these. Thank you."

"How much do I owe you for the meal?" Slocum asked. Jorge poured more coffee into Slocum's cup.

"*No importa*," Jorge said. "You do not pay."

"I still don't know why you were allowed to open this café and earn money here."

"Scud said he needed someone to cook the Mexican food. He said he wanted his Mexican men to have a place to eat in town, but not at the hotel. So he said he needed me and for that favor I pay him very dearly."

Slocum struck a match and lit their cheroots. The two men sat and smoked.

"Where will you get the guns?" Jorge asked after a few minutes of savoring the cigar. He beckoned to Esperanza with his hand and she came over. "*Traiganos un cenicero*," he said to her.

"I will bring the ashtray," she replied in English, then wafted away like a graceful dancer gliding across a stage.

"I don't know," Slocum said. "I was going to talk to the gunsmith when he opens his shop."

"Ah, Tim Chandler, yes. I know him. He, too, is a prisoner here in Polvo."

"How so?"

"He told me that Scud offered him a job and brought him here. He needed a gunsmith. But Tim did not want to stay, so Scud threatened to kill his family in Abilene if he did not stay. Tim is not a brave man, but he does know the guns."

"Maybe he might help me."

"I am going to tell you something, Mr. Slocum. I should not do this, but I feel that I can trust you."

"You can trust me, Jorge," Slocum said.

"My name is not Alessandro. I did not want Scud to know that I have two sons here at the diggings. Carlos and Mario. Our true last name is Benitez. They had guns when they came here, the pistols and the rifles. So did many others. Scud took them away and put them in a heavy vault."

"Do you know where this vault is?" Slocum asked. "A stick or two of dynamite might crack it open."

"Yes, I know where the vault is. It is in Tim's shop. But he must ask permission from Scud when he wants to take out a gun. Only Scud knows the combination."

"Scud thinks of damned near everything, doesn't he?" Slocum said.

"He thinks of much. But he cannot see into our hearts. He does not read our minds. I think that Fate brought you here, John Slocum. I think you are the messiah we have been praying for, hoping for."

"Hey, hold on there, Jorge. I'm no savior. I'm just fed up with the injustice I see here in this town and I want to help if I can."

"I will talk to Tim. Can you come back around ten o'clock to his gun shop?"

"I can and I will."

"You do not pay for the meal. I do. You must be careful when you are in town, though. There are many men who would shoot you in the back for the reward money. Two thousand dollars is a lot of money in Polvo."

"It's probably more than Scud and his men are worth all put together."

Jorge laughed and pulled on the cheroot. Slocum picked up his hat and stood up. He left two dollar bills on the table.

"For Esperanza," he said. "I'll see you at ten o'clock, Jorge."

"Ten cuidado," Jorge said as Slocum walked to the door.

Slocum knew what the Mexican meant.

Be careful.

The morning was in full bloom when Slocum walked back to where he had left Ferro. He patted his belly and drew smoke into his throat and lungs. It was a fine morning. It was a morning full of hope and promise.

But when he rounded the corner, he stopped dead in his tracks.

There was a man standing in the shade of an overhang where Ferro was hitched. He was smoking a cigarette.

Slocum recognized him.

This was the skinny man who had braced him near the diggings, near the little pueblo where the Mexican workers were held as virtual prisoners. Slocum ground the rest of his cheroot underfoot and walked toward the man, his right hand just touching the butt of his pistol.

The man held one of the flyers in his hand.

But he wasn't looking at it. He was smoking that cigarette and blowing smoke into the air and watching it whisk away in the wind.

19

Slocum walked along the length of the closed shops while the thin man looked up at the smoke he blew from his mouth. He didn't appear to be a man on the lookout for a fugitive or a wanted man with a price on his head.

"You waiting for somebody?" Slocum said in a low tone of voice as he came within five feet of the man leaning against a storefront.

The cigarette dropped from the man's hand and he seemed to jump half a foot. His face bore a look of surprise and his hands started shaking. He dropped the flyer, too, and it fluttered to the ground at his feet.

"You figuring to make yourself a little extra money, feller?" Slocum said in his gruffest voice as the startled man's face blanched and his legs shook so much that his trousers rippled like a defective windsock.

"Un, no, not rightly, ah, Mr. Slocum. I—I just wanted to talk to you real bad. Is there someplace we can go where nobody's a-goin' to see us?"

"I'm heading for the livery stable. You can bring your horse and tie him up there."

"That'd be fine, Mr. Slocum. I don't mean to cause you no harm and I ain't after that reward."

"That's what you say," Slocum said.

"I mean it, sir. I didn't know who you was when I braced you out at the diggings. I truly didn't."

"How'd you find out? By looking at that wanted dodger?"

The two men untied their horses and walked up the street, which was still quiet at that hour. A few people were unlocking their stores and others were sweeping out dust through open doors.

"No, sir. The men who come out to relieve us told us all about you makin' the sheriff strip down buck naked and lockin' him up in the hoosegow. They thought you was pretty bold."

"They tell you I shot his deputy?"

"Yes, sir, they did, but they also said that the deputy killed Gloria up in her crib. They said you shot him square between the eyes."

Slocum said nothing, but as the stable came into sight, he walked toward the back. The sheriff's office was still dark and plastered with those wanted posters.

"When I heard all that, I didn't say nothin' 'bout you bein' out there. They might have reported me to Scud for lettin' you get away."

"Smart," Slocum said.

They reached the back corral and Slocum tied his reins to one of the cross poles. The slim man did the same.

"Say, feller, what's your name anyway? You know mine. I don't know yours."

"My name's Delbert Crowell. Most call me Del."

"All right, Del, tell me why you wanted to talk to me. You could get into a lot of trouble with Scud, you know."

"I know, but he's the reason I come a-lookin' for you. When I saw your horse there, I knew you'd be by to get it and so I just waited."

"All right. You found me. Now what do you want?"

"Well, sir, I ain't happy workin' for Scud and I feel sorry for all them Messicans. I mean I see 'em every night and they look so damned poorly and I know how they live and what Scud makes 'em do ever' day. It's a cryin' shame."

"Why don't you just leave, Del?"

"Last man what tried to leave was brought back and hanged from a pole right in the middle of town. But he was already shot in both kneecaps and his face was all puffy from bein' beaten half to death. No, sir, I warn't goin' to run away and get my neck stretched. No way."

"Why come to see me, then?"

The two men walked through the gate and over to the small door at the rear of the stable. There, Slocum paused to hear Del's answer.

"I figured on my ride back into town that if you stood up to Sheriff Scudder, you might be the one to help me get out of this hellhole."

"What makes you think that?" Slocum asked.

"Hell, I saw the way you didn't back down and knew you wasn't bluffin' when I come up on you out at the 'dobe town. I figured you was a man to ride the river with and I wanted to sound you out about Scud and his brother. See if you was goin' to light a shuck or stay and fight. Then I saw that dodger and I knowed you was not on Scud's side."

Slocum opened the door and they walked inside. Some of the horses nickered and they heard the sound of someone cleaning out one of the stalls.

"Wait here a minute," Slocum said, and left Del there by the door while he walked down to the open stall.

Inside, a young man with a shovel was scooping up horse droppings and straw and dumping the refuse into a small wheelbarrow.

"You Ralston?" Slocum said.

The man froze with the shovel in midair and turned to look at Slocum.

"Yeah, I'm Lew Ralston. You got a horse here?"

"I'm Joe Wilson," Slocum said.

"No, you ain't."

"What?"

"Hell, I seen your picture nailed up all over town. Caleb said you was Wilson, but I know better."

"What else did he tell you, kid?"

"I ain't no kid, Mr. Slocum, and you're a wanted man. Got a bounty on your head."

"You care to try and collect it, Ralston?"

"No, sir. You can see I ain't got no gun and I sure don't want no trouble. Just go on about your business here and I won't get in your hair."

"That's good to know, Ralston. You keep shoveling shit and we'll get along."

"Yes, sir. You need anything, you just holler, hear?"

"I'm going to get some of my gear out of the loft and I may be back later."

"You go right ahead sir. I got to clean out all these stalls."

Slocum walked back to where Del was standing.

"You wait here. I'm going up in the loft and I won't be long."

"I ain't in no hurry to go nowhere," Del said.

Slocum climbed into the loft and saw that Fanny was dressing. She stood in front of a small window, a silhouette limned with rays of sunlight.

"I wondered where you were, John," she said. "I woke up and you were gone."

"I've got to find a place for you to stay. Mind a little walk through town?"

"I'd rather stay here with you and do it one more time," she said, a coquettish lilt to her voice.

"Some other time," he said. He bent down to roll up his bedroll. He picked up his rifle and tucked the bedroll under his left arm, then grabbed his saddle. Fanny finished putting on her shoes and fluffing her hair.

"Let's go," he said, and the two walked to the ladder and

climbed down it. Ralston was still in the same stall and they could hear him chunking horse offal into the wheelbarrow. He was whistling some old song that neither of them knew.

Del looked surprised when the two walked out of the shadows.

"You got a woman here?" Del said.

"One of those Scud kidnapped. Del, this is Fanny Beeson. Fanny, this is Del Crowell."

"Pleased to meetcha," Fanny said.

"Me, too," Del said.

The three of them walked outside and over to the horses. Slocum slung the saddle over his horse, secured it in place. After he slid his rifle into its scabbard and tied his bedroll on the back of the saddle, he looked over at Del, who was standing next to Ferro's rump.

"Del, do you live alone?" Slocum asked.

"Well, yeah, I do. I built me a little shack over on Third Street. Why?"

"Fanny. She needs a place to stay. A place to hide where she'll be safe until I clear up some things in town."

"You mean you want me to take her in?"

"Just for a few days. If you think she'd be safe there."

"I was hopin' to throw in with you, Mr. Slocum. I don't want to guard them poor Messicans no more."

"That's a pretty big decision, Del."

"I know it is. I'm just about to the end of my rope, Mr. Slocum."

"Call me John, will you. I keep thinking you're talking to my father."

"Sure, John."

"Well, let's see where you live, and if you have any food there, I'm sure Fanny would be mighty grateful if you were to feed her."

"Don't I have any say in this?" Fanny asked.

Slocum looked at her, a quizzical expression on his face.

"Seems to me that you don't have too many choices,

Fanny," Slocum said. "If Scudder or Scud sees you on the street, you'll be right back in their grimy clutches."

"That's another thing, Mr., ah, John, about Scud and his brother," Delbert said.

"What's that?" Slocum asked.

"I found out them two and some others done left town early this mornin'," the boy replied.

"Do you know where they were going?" Slocum asked.

"Yes, sir, I do. I been out there with them before. They always go there when they have some dirty work to do and don't want to get none of it on their hands."

"Where is that, Del?"

"Why, over to the Injun camp. They's a little bunch of Kiowa camped about five miles from here. Scud takes 'em likker and sometimes ammunition and grub. I drove a wagon out there once't or twice and the smell of them Injuns just about blowed me off my feet."

Slocum grinned and gave Del a look that would melt an unlit candle.

"Del, I could kiss you," Slocum said.

Del backed away and held up both hands palms out.

"Don't you be doin' nothin' like that, John," Del said.

"Just joking. Let's take Fanny to your place and get her settled, then you come with me. We've got work to do. If you want to see this town cleaned up and get yourself out from under Scud's yoke, that is."

"I sure do," Del said, and he grinned wide, showing his tobacco-stained teeth.

"Well, I hope this man Del has a nice place and you don't keep me there too long," Fanny said.

"Your choice," Slocum said, tiring of her demanding ways.

"Oh, all right. I guess I'll go and hide out."

Slocum helped her up to a perch behind the cantle and then climbed into the saddle.

"Lead the way, Del," Slocum said as the man stepped

into his stirrups and swung into the saddle. "We've got a hell of a lot to do after we get Fanny settled."

"Yes, sir. I feel real good about that, John."

Slocum followed Del as he rode to the next street then turned toward the east, where the sun was blazing in a nearly cloudless sky. People were starting to appear on the street—shop owners, as well as merchants with their mule- and burro-drawn carts laden with fabrics, pottery, and gewgaws all probably handmade and sold cheap.

Slocum drew his hat brim down and lowered his head as they rode past all the wanted flyers nailed to walls and posts along their way.

He felt better about one thing, though.

Scud and his brother were not in town. He could breathe a little easier, but he knew he still had to be on guard. There were men in Polvo who would not think twice about shooting him in the back. They were the wild cards in a deck full of jokers.

He had sat at this table many times before.

And he had played this same game with a table full of cardsharps.

20

Del's house stood on four concrete pillars. A mangy black dog had burrowed a bed for itself under the house at one of the corners. It rose from its bed and chased two sparrows that were hopping across the barren yard.

"That's Sassy," Del said. "Not my dog, but she's adopted me."

"Oh, sweet," Fanny said.

Slocum was surprised to see a small hitching post made out of wagon springs welded together on one side of the house at the end of the street. The house itself was framed with whipsawed lumber and appeared very sturdy with a roof made out of froed shakes, unlike the others nearby, which were constructed of a combination of adobe brick and uneven slabs of knotty pine.

"Nice house," Slocum said.

Del looked sheepish as he dismounted near the odd-looking hitching post. He wrapped his reins around one of the springs and took Slocum's reins and wrapped those on the opposite part of the T.

"I was a carpenter back in Del Rio," he said. "I scrounged

around for the lumber to build this place at a sawmill down in Alpine."

"So, you came here of your own free will," Slocum said as he dismounted and helped Fanny light down.

"Saw an ad in the San Antone paper offering carpenter work and asking for a load of lumber."

"And what happened when you got here?"

"I hauled lumber up here and Scud offered me a job, said I could build me a house with the lumber I brought. Said he would make me rich if I helped him mine silver and gold out at that big old ravine. Only gold I seen since was on a ring he wears on his finger."

"But you couldn't leave," Slocum said.

"Threatened to kill me if I tried."

"And you believed him."

"I believed him when he showed me the little cemetery out yonder," Del said. "He said the men who were buried there had all tried to light a shuck for other parts and wound up in Boot Hill."

Fanny gasped as Del led them all to the house. The door was unlocked and they walked inside. It was a large one-room dwelling with a pair of small cubicles, one of which had a cot where Del slept. The other was a storage room with nail kegs and a wall holding hammers, saws, and chisels.

"I like to keep my hand in. Build furniture I sell to the Mexes in town when I ain't workin' as a guard out at the 'dobe town. Miss Fanny, you can sleep on that there cot. I got a little bed out back. I generally like to sleep under the stars. It's cooler there. I got a little kitchen out back, too, that I'm framin' in, but it's got a woodstove and skillet, wash bowls and such."

Fanny walked through the room and out the back door.

"It ain't much," Del said, "but I like to tinker and I was a-goin' to add me another room later on. I been storin' up old wagon sheets and side boards from broke-down rigs out at the diggings."

Fanny returned after a few moments.

She was beaming.

"What a charming little kitchen you got, Del. I mean, it's got cabinets and a larder and a nice little cookstove. You got a pantry and was that a well I saw out back?"

"Shore was," Del said. "Bricked in with 'dobes I got from the Mexes in town."

"It looks like a wishing well, with its little shake roof and the rope and bucket."

Del held up his hands.

"All these nicks and scrapes prove I done built most everything you see," he said.

"I'll be just fine here, John. But don't make me wait too long. I know you got things to do."

"I hope to bring your friends back here right quick," Slocum said. "Especially Melissa. If I can find her."

"I'm counting on you, John," she said. Then she ring-necked him with both arms and planted a juicy smack on his lips. She broke the embrace and started for Del, who retreated, holding up both hands to ward her off. His face took on a rosy hue and Fanny laughed.

"Shoo," she said with a smile, and waved the men out the door.

The two men left and mounted their horses, rode back to town. They went straight to the gun shop. Jorge was waiting for them outside, talking to Tim, a gray-haired man in his early fifties, with a silver moustache and fluffy white sideburns. He wore horn-rimmed eyeglasses and a striped shirt made of muslin that had been recently redyed with a bluish tint.

Del and Slocum dismounted and tied their horses to the hitch rail.

Jorge introduced the gunsmith to Del and Slocum. The three men shook hands.

"Let's go inside," Tim said, looking around furtively. There were a few people on the street, and most of the small shops were open. But it was still quiet in their vicinity, and no one seemed to be gawking at them. The four men entered the gun shop. Slocum adjusted his eyes to the light and saw that he was in a large workroom. There were just a few guns on display, rifles leaning on racks against the wall, a couple of old percussion pistols hanging from dowels by their trigger guards, and an old pirate's flintlock pistol in a frame attached to the wall.

There was a long worktable with a metal lathe at one end, a hurricane lamp in the center near one edge, and various tools arranged next to a Henry rifle, which was broken down into various sections: barrel, stock, receiver, lever, and magazine.

"Jorge told me who you were, Slocum, and said that you could be trusted. Find yourselves stools and set down."

There were several small stools arranged around an unlit potbellied stove and a wood box full of kindling and wood scraps.

The men sat down.

"I'd like to see that vault you have here. I understand it's full of old rifles and pistols."

Slocum pulled out a cheroot and offered it to Tim.

"I don't smoke," Tim said. "I keep powder in the back room, where I do reloading and make up cartridges for various calibers of rifles and pistols."

"Then I won't smoke either," Slocum said.

"I appreciate that. One stray spark and this place would go up like a volcano."

"About that vault," Slocum repeated.

"Ain't really a vault. More like a big safe, but it's locked tight. Might be a tough nut to crack."

"How many guns do you have in there?" Slocum asked.

"Maybe three dozen rifles and scatterguns, twice that many pistols, none of 'em new or worth havin' in my estimation. There are some Colts, a Paterson or two, some Smith and Wessons, a few converted Navys and Armys, a derringer, some Remingtons, both percussion and conversions. Like the New Model Army with a top strap."

"I'm familiar with most of them. Will they shoot?"

"I reckon. I keep some black powder and percussion caps in my little safe back there, some 3F and 2F powder."

"Just in case, eh?" Slocum said.

Tim grinned. "A cap and ball kills just as good as a percussion Colt," Tim said.

"You know what I want the guns for, Tim?"

"No, I don't. Jorge just said you was interested."

"How would you feel if I got a bunch of Mexicans together, those who work out at the diggings, and gave them arms?"

Tim scratched a small furrow in his gray hair.

"I'd say you was plumb loco, Mr. Slocum."

"Why?" Slocum said.

"Scud and his men pack the latest Colts and Winchesters. Most of 'em are crack shots and they sure don't mind shootin' Mexes, nor anybody else who bucks 'em."

"I can arm about a dozen men, and with Del here and my own weapons, I think we can even up the odds at least."

"Scud, he has many men who work for him," Jorge said.

"Yeah, he does," Del added. "At least two dozen, by my count."

"Any of them likely to throw in with us, Del?" Slocum asked.

Del shook his head.

"I wouldn't trust none of 'em. Yesterday I wouldn't have trusted myself."

Tim looked at Del in surprise.

"You must be loco, too," Tim said.

"I reckon I am, but when I run into Slocum here, I figgered he wasn't a man to back down no matter what and I'm sick of workin' for Scud and Oren. When I look at them poor Mexes slavin' long days in those diggings, I can't hardly live with my conscience."

Tim rocked back and forth on his stool, as if that triggered some mechanism in his mind that instigated serious thought.

"Lessen you can get the combination to that gun safe from Scud, Slocum, you'll have to blow it. And I don't want to be around when you do it."

Slocum looked at Del.

"I saw boxes of dynamite out at the diggings. Also caps and fuses. Think we can rustle up some of that to use on that safe, Del?"

"At night the guards don't watch over the diggings, so it wouldn't be hard to grab some of those sticks and the fixin's, I reckon."

"All right. Tim, we'll get the dynamite tonight and blow the safe around midnight, if that's all right. You might have to move your powder."

"I'll have it out of here by nightfall," Tim said. "You want to take a look at that safe?"

"Yes. I don't want to blow your building down, but I need to see what I'm facing."

The men got up with a scraping of stool legs on the hardwood floor. Tim led them through a door to another room. There, in the center, was a very large safe with a wheel lock in the center.

"You have a drill with a large bit, Tim?" Slocum asked.

"An inch bit is all. Be hard as hell to drill though that steel, though."

Slocum walked up to the safe and gripped the wheel. It did not turn when he applied pressure to it. He walked around the safe. It was at least four feet deep and over five foot in height. There was a gap between the bottom and the floor. The safe was on large iron casters so that it could be rolled if need be. He got down on his belly and reached a hand under the safe and felt the bottom of it.

He crawled backward and stood up.

"Might not need to drill," he said.

"Why not?" Tim asked.

Slocum ran his fingers around the seam in the door.

"You got glue here?" he asked Tim. "Strong glue?"

"I got glue, strong as blacksmith's glue. Why?"

"I'll need some. I have an idea how we can blow the door off this safe and not damage any of the weapons inside."

"You a powder man?" Tim asked.

"I've handled dynamite before," Slocum said. "I have a hell of a lot of respect for it and Mr. Du Pont."

"I wish you luck," Chandler said.

"Luck depends on planning, Tim," Slocum said. "I'm a man who takes kindly to planning."

"I'm glad to hear that," Tim said.

"See you sometime after midnight, Tim," Slocum said.

"No, you won't. I'll be at the Desert Rose. The door to my shop will be unlocked. Just come on in and do what you have to do."

"All right. I don't blame you. But why go to the saloon?"

"Because if anything goes wrong, I want plenty of witnesses who will swear I was drinking at the bar and not touching off dynamite in my own shop."

Slocum laughed.

Del frowned and Jorge nodded with approval.

Slocum and Chandler shook hands.

"Thanks," Slocum said.

"You'll need a wagon to haul all those guns out of here if you do blow that safe," Tim said.

Slocum looked at Del.

"They's wagons out at the diggin's," he said. "I reckon we can hook one up and drag it here."

"Problem solved," Slocum said. He looked at Jorge. "Thanks, Jorge," he said. "Wish me luck."

"*Suerte, amigo,*" Jorge said. "*Vaya con Dios.*"

"I'll go with Del, Jorge. God can tag along after us."

Jorge laughed. Del didn't get the joke.

The two men walked out to their horses. Before they mounted up, they spoke in low tones.

"Do you know who will be on night guard out at the adobe village, Del?"

"I'm supposed to be one of 'em, but there should be two men working."

"Do I have to worry about them when we go after the dynamite and haul that wagon out?"

"We might have do some work before we steal the dynamite and the wagon, John."

"You mean unsaddle them?"

"I mean shoot 'em plumb dead. One of 'em is Faron Lawrence, a gunslinger from Waco, and the other'n is Jubal Gaston, from New Orleans, a back-shootin' thief from way back. Handpicked by Scud and who do most of the killin' around here."

"Handpicked, huh?"

"Yes, sir, handpicked for pure meanness."

"Well, then, we'll just have to unpick them, won't we?"

"Won't be so easy in the dark. Them two are hard to sneak up on."

"Well, so is an elk or a deer," Slocum said. "And unless these men have great big ears and a mighty keen sense of smell, I think I can manage a good stalk."

Del said nothing. Slocum could see that he wasn't convinced. Del knew the men and Slocum did not. But he had met such men before.

Slocum had fought with Quantrill during the war. He knew how to do battle with the enemy.

And besides, he thought. It was two against two. Those were fair odds in his book.

21

Slocum knew he was taking a big chance by returning to the Desert Rose Saloon. It was a risk he was willing to take as long as he had Del with him to point out any of Scud's gunslingers. He didn't want to walk in cold, though, so he and Del left their horses hitched well away from the saloon and separate. They stood across the street from the saloon a long while, watching who went in and came out.

"Most of the men who work for Scud come in the through the back door, but he don't usually have nobody but the bartenders and the glitter gals a-workin'."

"Just tell me if you see any of the men you know going into the saloon," Slocum said.

"You aimin' to take them gals out tonight?"

"No, I just want to see them first. Especially Melissa. See if she's started work in there."

"I could go in and check for you," Del offered.

"Just watch my back when we go in," Slocum said.

Several men and a few women on their arms went into the saloon over the next hour, but none were packing sidearms.

There were several Mexicans and single white men who looked more like farm boys than gunslingers.

"All right," Slocum said. "I've seen enough. You go in first and see that I have a stool at this end of the bar near the doors. I'll come in about five minutes later."

"Looks like the usual crowd to me," Del said.

"If you say so."

They could hear the lively music from the band as Del walked across the street and parted the batwing doors. A few more men in pairs and trios walked in, and then Slocum made his move.

There was an empty stool at the end of the bar, and Jack Akers was serving a man about midway down the bar. So Slocum slipped onto the stool and waited to catch the barkeep's attention. A few stools away sat Del, a beer in front of him. He did not nod to Slocum but assumed an air of complete indifference when Slocum scanned the others at the bar, which included Del.

He saw Jack pouring a drink for a new arrival, then turned to look out over the tables. He saw a tall graceful woman wearing the outfit of a glitter gal, and another, shorter, but just as pretty. At the far end, he caught a glimpse of Melissa. She was smiling and patronizing a middle-aged gentleman who looked like a banker, with his gray suit, brownish-gold vest, and dangling watch chain. The top of his balding head shone like a small moon under the candlelit chandelier.

Akers approached and stood looking at Slocum.

"I guess it's no more Mr. Wilson, is it, Slocum?" Akers said.

"Take your pick, Jack."

"You got more nerve than my mother-in-law, Slocum."

"That's Mr. Slocum to you, Jack," Slocum said.

"My mistake. But after last night, I never expected to see you again. Some Kentucky bourbon, Mr. Slocum?"

"Not tonight, Jack. Just draw me a beer. Any kind. I'm not particular."

"I guess it's good for you that Sheriff Scudder is not in town tonight."

"I'm always grateful for small favors," Slocum said.

As Jack turned to pour Slocum a beer, Slocum called to him. "Have Melissa come over here when she's not too busy, will you?"

"Sure," Akers said, and gave a signal to Melissa at the back of the room.

Apparently, she had been trained, like the other girls, to keep an eye on the bartenders for just such requests. The Mexican girl slinked by at a nearby table and gave Slocum the eye. He winked at her and she winked back.

Slocum saw Melissa leave her table and walk slowly toward the bar, smiling at those patrons she passed, who all looked up at her with admiring glances.

Akers set a beer down in front of Slocum.

"Two bits," he said.

Slocum put a quarter on the bartop.

"I'm supposed to show you a flyer," Akers said. "But I reckon you already know you got a price on your head. Scudder's hoppin' mad."

"I've had a price on my head a good long time, Jack," Slocum said.

"One thousand of that two thousand is bein' put up by Scud. He wants to tack your hide to the barn door and set the door on fire."

"You're a regular information bureau, Jack. Maybe you ought to think about starting up a newspaper."

"Here's your gal, Slocum. Buy her a drink or she's gone to greener pastures."

"Bring her what she wants," Slocum said as Melissa sidled up and sat down on an empty stool.

"Buy me a drink, John?" she said. "That's what they told me to say to anyone who wants to talk to me."

"On the way, Melissa."

"Well, how do I look?" she said.

"You look like a two-bit whore," he said, keeping his voice low.

She reacted as if he had slapped her.

"That's not a nice thing to say, John."

"You asked. Don't tell me you like working here."

"Scud was real nice to me. He told me I could make a lot of money and that he would put most of it into a savings account for me in case I ever wanted to leave Polvo or get married."

"And you believed him?"

"Sure. Why not?"

"Scud is a damned liar."

Akers brought a glass that looked like whiskey but Slocum knew was mostly tea. He set it down and Slocum dug out two one-dollar bills and laid them on the counter. Akers snatched up the bills and started to walk back to his station at the bar's center.

"If you or the other barkeep even reach for a weapon, you'll wind up in a pine box, Jack."

"Scudder will take care of you when he gets back in town. Or so he said."

"No reward for you, then," Slocum said.

"That's the luck of the draw, Slocum."

Akers walked away, a slight swagger to his gait.

"I saw the flyers, John," Melissa said. "You killed some judge, didn't you?"

Slocum shrugged.

"That shoe don't fit," he said, assuming his Georgia drawl as if he had just left the farm.

"Who's the tall gal?" Slocum asked. He sipped his beer and inclined his head toward one of the glitter gals.

"That's Darla. Darla Whipple. The other one is Susan Lindale. I don't know where Fanny is. Darla said she escaped last night."

"Had any paying customers yet?"

"I don't know what you mean, John."

"They give you a crib upstairs?"

"A small room. We don't have to take customers up there. Scud said we could use it on our breaks and sleep over if we got too tired. He's given us a nice little adobe house. Anita Gonzales stays there and that other Mexican gal who works here, Florita. I forget her last name."

"You heard what happened to Gloria last night, didn't you? She worked here, too."

"I didn't know her. Anita said she died."

"Scudder's deputy blew her to pieces with a sawed-off shotgun loaded with buckshot."

"I didn't know that," she said.

"There's a lot you don't know, Melissa. But I wanted to warn you about what they say about dogs and people."

"What's that?"

"You lie down with dogs and you get fleas. If you had the chance to get out of town, would you take it?"

"I'd have to think about it," she said.

"You mean you're willing to be one of Scud's whores?"

"I'm not a whore, John. I just serve drinks and talk to the customers, make them feel at home."

"That costume you're wearing says different."

"Oh, John, you act like a damned prude. This is fun for me after what I've been through. You should be happy for me. I'm going to make a lot of money and meet a nice man who will marry me. That's just what I came to Texas for."

Slocum drank half the beer in his glass. He looked over at Del, who was straining with all his might to hear what Slocum was saying. He turned away as soon as Slocum looked at him.

"I don't think you'll have this job long," Slocum said.

"Why not?"

"I don't think Scud and his crooked brother, the sheriff, are going to be around long enough to pay your salary."

"I get tips, too," she said, and patted her boobies. They crackled with the sound of paper money.

"Just giving a word to the wise," Slocum said.

"You going to shoot Scud and his brother?"

"If I get the chance."

"They're too smart for you, John. Scud is the toughest man I ever met. I mean, he's hard inside and out. He owns practically this whole town and men have tried to kill him before. Anita told me that and I believe her. She said Scud was dangerous and that I should not make him angry."

"That was probably good advice, Melissa."

"But I don't want you to get hurt either, John. You were nice to me and I'm grateful to you for what you done."

Slocum finished his beer, set down the empty glass.

"I wish you luck, Melissa," he said. "Don't end up like Gloria."

"I won't," she said. "Good-bye, John. I don't know what you're up to, but I think you're in way over your head."

"That's when a man does his best swimming," he said. "When he's in over his head."

She gave him a pitying look and slid off the bar stool. She assumed an air of friendliness and enthusiasm as she strutted back to the tables, smiling and curtsying at every ogling drinker.

Slocum nodded to Del and held up two fingers.

"Two minutes," he said without voicing the words, and got up from his stool. He walked out the batwing doors and onto the street.

Two or three minutes later, Del joined him.

"Is that it, John? What now?"

"Now, we go out to the diggings."

"That was a mighty pretty gal you was talkin' to in there."

"She's a lost soul, I'm afraid," Slocum said.

"I saw two other new gals just as pretty and warn't none of 'em lookin' too lost to me."

"Scud fed them a pack of lies and they think they've found a home in that saloon."

"Scud's that way."

"Did he tell you he would put part of your pay into a savings account that you could draw out if you ever wanted to leave?"

"Why, he shore as hell did. Most of my pay goes into the bank."

"Ever try to draw out any of that money, Del?"

Del scratched his head as he untied his horse.

"Come to think of it, I never did. But I calculate it's better'n four hundred dollars by now."

"Anybody you know ever try and take out their savings?"

"Well, Charlie Fields, he did once."

"And did he get his money?"

"I don't rightly now. Maybe. They said he left town to buy him a ranch or something."

"I wonder how far he got," Slocum said.

"What do you mean?"

"I mean Charlie's probably lying in that graveyard outside of town, feeding the worms."

"Shit, John, you don't know that for sure."

"No, I don't, Del. I just know one thing."

"What's that?" Del asked.

"It seems to me that a lot of people have come to this town, by hook or by crook."

"Yeah, probably true," Del said as he climbed into the saddle. Slocum hauled himself aboard Ferro and looked over at Del.

"People come here and nobody leaves town alive," Slocum said as he turned Ferro out into the street.

Del didn't answer, but when he rode alongside, Slocum could see that he was thinking about what Slocum had said.

He was thinking real hard.

And counting on his fingers. He got all the way to one finger.

But, Slocum thought, he didn't seem to be too sure about that piece of arithmetic.

22

The town died a few minutes after they rode away from the saloon. The town was dark and lifeless, its streets empty, its buildings silent, as if some plague wave had wafted through it, wiping out all its inhabitants. They rode out onto the desolate starlit plain with its shadowy shapes, its jumble of rocks and grotesque plants that seemed like mutations of animals alien to this planet or any other.

Del veered off to their left.

"Best we circle up behind the diggin's," he said. "We'll have a better chance at that dynamite."

"Good idea," Slocum said. "I'll follow you."

They didn't even see the adobe pueblo but arrived on the far side of the ravine, where Del halted his horse.

"We'll just wait here a few minutes to see if we got company," he whispered.

Moonlight dusted them as it rose and spread its dim frost on the deserted ravine, the tools and supplies on the other side. The bowels of the ravine were pitch dark and smelled of burnt powder and wet clay, musty broken rocks, and the faint aroma of mule droppings and urine.

"You think one of those guards might come out this way?" Slocum said *sotto voce*. Ferro tossed his head and pawed the ground as if wondering why they were not moving and perhaps smelling what scents wafted from that dark hole in the earth a few yards away.

"If they suspicion anyone's prowlin' around out here, they could ride up, I reckon. Don't expect 'em to."

Slocum said nothing. Instead, he scanned the lumpy shadows that were the tools under tarps and the wagons that were standing at various places along the length of the flat above the ravine. A bullbat whispered past them, and in the distance a lone coyote yapped then went silent. They heard no sounds from the adobe village, nor did they hear hoof-beats or the clink of an iron shoe on stone.

"Pretty quiet," Del said, his voice barely audible.

"Do we ride down there or stay on the plain and go to the other side?"

"Be quieter if we ride around. Real slow like."

"I'll go as slow as you do," Slocum said.

They rode very slowly to the head of the ravine, rounded it, and headed for the place where the dynamite was stored. There they dismounted and tied their reins to a long log used for shoring up a mine shaft.

Del reached down and pulled back the tarp. He pulled it slowly so that it wouldn't crackle or make any other noise. There, stacked, were wood boxes of Du Pont 60/40 dynamite. There were smaller boxes of caps and coils of coated fuses.

Slocum looked over at the nearest wagon and pointed to it.

Del nodded.

Slocum picked up a box of dynamite and carried it over to the wagon. He placed it gently on the bed near the front. Del came over with a box of blasting caps and a twenty-five-foot coil of fuse. He laid them next to the box of dynamite.

"What else?" he asked.

"That should do it," Slocum said. "Now do we hook our horses up to the wagon or find us some mules?"

"The mules are kept in a corral at one end of the 'dobe town," he said. "Be hard to get 'em with those guards ridin' back and forth all night."

"And if we hook up our horses, we'll be at a disadvantage when we leave here. The wagon will make a lot of noise. So I have a better idea."

Slocum climbed up into the wagon, took his knife out, and slid it under the lid of the dynamite box. He pried the lid off.

"Look in my saddlebags, Del, and bring me my gloves. I don't want to handle this stuff without protection."

"How come?" Del asked.

"Those dynamite sticks have some kind of coating on them. You get it on your hands and then rub your head, you're going to have the worst headache in the world. I mean a real bad headache that might blind you for two or three days."

"I didn't know that," Del said.

"Get the gloves."

Del rummaged around in both of Slocum's saddlebags until he found a pair of heavy work gloves. He handed them to Slocum, who put them on.

"Now bring me my saddlebags," he said. "Then get yours."

"I see what you're doin'," Del said. "We don't need no wagon."

"Not now, but if and when we get those guns out of that safe, we might need a wagon to lug them all out to the Mexicans."

Del returned with Slocum's saddlebags, then went to retrieve his own. Slocum picked up three sticks of dynamite and placed them in the bottom of one bag. Then he picked up three more and put them in the other bag.

He handed Del the box of caps and the coil of fuse.

"Pack those down tight," he said. "One of those caps can blow your hand off."

"Why did you change your mind about takin' the wagon?" Del asked.

"I figured to use the wagon to load up those weapons when we blew the safe. Then I realized that it not only would be unnecessary, but we'd lose the use of our horses. Plus, there are wagons and carts in town. We're still going to need men to use those rifles and pistols. I'll need José Delgado to help me with manpower."

"Who's José Delgado?" Del asked.

"He's one of the workers. If I can, I'd like to bring him with us."

"That might be tough, with those two guards prowling around the 'dobes."

"Maybe not," Slocum said enigmatically.

"You mean to take 'em out? Tonight?"

"It's a matter of chance, Del."

"Chance?"

"If I get the chance, I'll take one or both guards down and that's two less of Scud's men to worry about."

Del swore under his breath.

Slocum added three more sticks of dynamite to each of his bags, then climbed out of the wagon. He put the saddlebags behind his saddle and let out a long breath.

Del finished with his saddlebags and then both men froze as they heard a sound.

"Shh," Slocum warned. He went into a crouch, his gun hand floating just above his pistol. He peered into the darkness.

Del froze. His face blanched with fear, turned ghostly white in the soft glare of moonlight.

Crunch, crunch.

They both heard it. Some animal walking over the rocks. A horse, perhaps.

Out of the shadows, they saw a looming figure on horse-back, the glint of light glancing off a rifle barrel.

"Who the hell's out there?" the man on horseback called out.

"That's Jubal Gaston," whispered Del, loud enough for Slocum to hear him. "Look out."

Jubal reined up his horse and stared straight at them. Both Slocum and Del were hunched down and the wagon was blocking Jubal's view. But Slocum knew he could see their horses and that was more than enough for the guard to know something was wrong.

Slocum held his breath.

Then he saw the rifle move and heard a click as the rider jacked a cartridge into the firing chamber.

Jubal raised his rifle to his shoulder, slowly, and then sighted down the barrel. He was deliberate in his actions, sure of himself.

In that moment, time stretched into an agonizing eternity, as if that single moment would last beyond memory, would remain fixed in Slocum's mind like some ancient, incom-prehensible relic that had been dug up and put on permanent display in a museum.

He let out his breath very slowly and the sound was like a ghostly whisper from some far-off place outside his own body.

23

In that split-second just before Gaston's rifle butt touched his shoulder, Slocum, almost without thinking, jerked his pistol from its holster.

His thumb pressed down on the hammer and the hammer clicked back into full cock as he brought the Colt up to fire.

Slocum knew that darkness distorted a man's vision, and that if he aimed for a small part of the man, he might miss. He might shoot high or low. So he centered the front sight on the rider's midsection, the largest part of the man in the saddle.

He aimed and he fired from both instinct and past experience. Fast as the speed of thought, he squeezed the trigger just as Gaston's rifle butt settled on the muscle of his shoulder.

As soon as Slocum fired, he hammered back for a second shot. Again, this was from both instinct and habit.

Flame, bright orange flame, spurted from the barrel of his pistol. He saw a wispy puff of smoke and then heard the smack of the bullet as it struck flesh. Gaston grunted and his torso twitched as the lead ball slammed him just below his rib cage, square above the belly's center. The rifle tumbled from his hands and clattered on the ground, unfired.

Gaston started to topple sideways from his saddle as blood rose up in his throat and spewed from his mouth like a black torrent, a single long gush that erupted from the volcano caused by the expanding lead bullet that smashed portions of his lungs and slammed into his spine with all the force of a sixteen-pound maul. His body contorted and he pitched forward over his saddle, his chest striking the saddle horn and causing his breath to drive more blood from his throat. Then he fell to one side and slipped out of the saddle. Gaston hit the ground with a loud thud and his gasping sounded like a blacksmith's bellows with a case of bronchitis.

Del cowered behind his horse for several seconds. Slocum stood up straight and walked over to the fallen man. He squatted down and touched the carotid artery with the tips of two fingers. He felt no pulse and Jubal lay stiff and still where he had fallen.

"He's dead, Del," Slocum said. "Come see for yourself."

Del walked over. He was hesitant, faltering in his slow gait. He seemed reluctant to look at the dead man.

Finally he said, "That's Jubal, all right. I didn't think he'd be so easy."

"It's never easy to kill a man, Del."

"I didn't mean it that way. I mean, one minute he was a big man on a tall horse and now he's just a bloody bag of bones."

"Strip off his gun belt and I'll get his rifle and any ammunition he has in his saddlebags."

"What you aim to do with Jubal's weapons?"

"I'm going to give them to José Delgado. Get that ball rolling."

"We still got Faron Lawrence to worry about. Likely he

heard that shot. Hell, they probably heard it clear over to Polvo."

Slocum picked up Jubal's rifle, while Del unbuckled the gun belt.

As Slocum was patting the withers of Jubal's gelding, he grabbed the reins and tied them to a wagon wheel.

"Likely José could use this horse, too," Slocum said. "It's a fine animal."

The horse was a sorrel gelding, standing at least fifteen or so hands high, and the saddle was out of Denver, with a roping horn, double-cinched. He rummaged through the saddlebags and came up with a box of .44-caliber pistol ammunition and a box of .30-caliber rifle cartridges. He left them in the saddlebags.

That was when they heard far-off hoofbeats. Somebody was riding hard down in the adobe barrio, and the sounds grew louder.

"He's a-comin' this way," Del whispered as he buckled Jubal's gun belt and slung it over one shoulder.

"Give me that," Slocum said.

Del handed him Jubal's rig and Slocum hung it from the saddle horn of the dead man's horse.

The hoofbeats grew louder.

"Now what do we do?" Del asked.

"We wait," Slocum said. "And listen."

They could hear the horse scramble up the slope toward the ravine. The rider was following the same path as Jubal had taken when he rode up on them.

They waited. And listened.

As the horse rounded the far end of the ravine and headed their way, Faron let out a shout.

"That you, Jubal? What's a-goin' on?"

"Yo," Slocum yelled and then smiled.

"Be right there," Faron yelled and the hoofbeats became louder as iron hooves pounded over dirt and gravel.

Del ducked down under the wagon. He drew his pistol but didn't cock it.

"Just hold on, Del. He's almost here."

Faron rode up, glancing at the two saddled horses, and then looked at Jubal's horse without seeing either Del or Slocum.

"Jubal, what in hell are you doin'?" Faron asked as he jerked his horse to a halt in a miniature cloud of dust that glistened with starlight then winked out so fast he seemed to be swallowed up by the night itself.

Slocum stepped out of the shadows, his right hand just touching the grip of his pistol.

"Throw up your hands, Lawrence," Slocum ordered.

"Who in the hell are you?" Faron said. He did not lift his arms or raise his hands.

"The name's Slocum. John Slocum."

A second or two passed as Faron Lawrence absorbed the name and worried it through the thick wool of his mind. His eyes were slitted, then opened wide.

"Why, you're the sonofabitch what's got a price on his head, the one who rousted Sheriff Scudder down at the saloon last night."

"The very same, Mr. Lawrence. Now climb down from your horse and keep your hands empty."

"You ain't orderin' me around, you two-bit bastard."

Faron's right hand plummeted to his holster. He clawed at the butt of his pistol, while fixing Slocum with a look of pure hatred.

Slocum pulled his pistol free of the holster. It was so smooth and fast that Faron appeared to hesitate for just a fraction of a second.

Then came the click of the hammer as Slocum cocked the Colt. His arm rose in a steady flow of movement as if he were setting up on a range for a target shoot and had all the time in the world.

Faron's pistol cleared leather, but his thumb slipped off the hammer in his haste to shoot first.

"You had your chance, Lawrence," Slocum said evenly as he squeezed the trigger. The Colt bucked against his palm and he thumbed the hammer back again, quicker than a man could count from one to two.

The pistol roared again and sprouted a column of fiery powder, propelling the lead pellet on a flat trajectory toward Faron's chest.

Faron jerked with a sudden spasm as the first bullet hit him in the left lung. A split second later a hole appeared where his heart pumped, just to the right of his breastbone. He tried to scream, but the noise that came out was so twisted and gravelly that it sounded like a dying crow's feeble squawk.

"You got him, John," Del cried out. "You got him."

Faron's eyes fixed in a death stare and seemed to gloss over with dull moonlight. His hand went limp and his pistol slipped from his grasp. He swayed slightly in the saddle before he just collapsed and tumbled off to one side.

His body made a dull sound as he hit the ground. His horse sidled away, its eyes rolling so that only the whites showed. It made a sound in its throat, a fearful nicker that rose to a thin squeal.

Slocum dug the toe of his boot under Faron's belly and kicked upward. Faron turned over on his back and stared up at him with eyes that had turned to a white frost. His mouth was slack and distended, and there was an almost imperceptible sag to his face as if his skin were melting into dry parchment.

"Strip off his gun belt and grab his horse," Slocum said. He opened the gate of his pistol and ejected two empty cartridges. He fed two fresh ones back into the cylinder and closed the gate. He spun the cylinder then eased the hammer between two of them and holstered his pistol.

He drew in a long breath and watched as Del took off the gun belt. Slocum led Faron's horse to the opposite side of the wagon and looped the reins around the wheel and a spoke.

"Now you got two horses and two rifles and two pistols to give to that Mex."

"It's a start," Slocum said. Then after he rubbed the sweat off the palms of his hands, he said, "Let's go see if José is ready to round up some men and ride into town."

"Think we need more dynamite, John?"

"We have enough to blow the safe."

"I'd like to blow up the whole town," Del said.

"It may come to that," Slocum said.

Del untied Faron's horse while Slocum took Jubal's reins. They rode around the ravine and down into the adobe village. Candles glowed in some of the huts, and by the time they reached José's, people were outside, speaking in Spanish whispers, questioning, wondering.

José stood outside as if he had been waiting for them. His eyes widened when he saw the two horses that he recognized as belonging to the night guards. Then he saw the rifles jutting from their scabbards and the pistols and gun belts dangling from the saddle horns.

"We heard the shots," he said. "You got their horses."

"We got their horses and they're yours, José. So are the guns. As for Faron and Jubal, you don't have to worry about them anymore. Now if you can round up one more man, you can ride into town with us tonight."

"What do we do in town?" José asked.

Slocum grinned.

"We're going to get you more guns and enough ammunition start a war."

"What?" José said.

"Listen to me, José," Slocum said. "I told you what you might have to do. There are men who would keep you poor and a prisoner here. There is no way to reason with them.

We are going to have to fight them. Kill them. Do you understand?"

"Yes, I will get Carlos Garcia to ride one of the horses. We will go with you to get the guns."

José went into the house, and they heard him explaining to his family in Spanish that he was leaving and that there would be fighting.

When he returned, he wore a straw hat and he walked to both horses, examined the pistols. Then he lifted Jubal's rig from the saddle horn and strapped on his gun belt.

"I am ready," he said. "We can pick up Carlos on our way."

"You catch on real fast, José," Slocum said as Delgado hoisted himself up in the saddle. Del handed him the reins of Faron's horse, and the three men rode off. People came out of their huts and offered encouragement and prayerful pronouncements. José grinned at all the attention.

Slocum looked up at the sky after Carlos had joined them and the four of them were riding toward Polvo. He gauged the moon's location and the Big Dipper.

"We'll make that midnight appointment, Del," he said.

"We should have dipped into that other box under the tarp," Del said.

"For what?"

"It has cotton to stuff in our ears when the dynamite goes off."

"Use your fingers," Slocum said.

Carlos, a short burly Mexican with a couple of gold teeth and a thin moustache, grinned.

"When I forget the cotton," he said, "I use the fingers."

Del laughed and they rode on.

Both José and Carlos drew their pistols and pointed them at imaginary targets several times. Then they pulled the rifles from their scabbards and aimed them at invisible targets as well.

Slocum watched them and wondered if they would have

the courage to fire their weapons at real men and watch them die. They were simple people and did not know much of murder or killing. But they were also oppressed people with a history of revolution in their country south of the border. So they knew what blood looked like and had seen so much poverty and cruelty at the hands of Scud's men that he was sure they were ready to overthrow the tyrant and cut down any man who stood in their way.

If they were not accustomed to killing, they would have to learn fast.

If not, he thought, they were all soon going to be dead men.

24

The street was deserted. The four men rode up to the gun shop and tied their horses to the hitch rails on the opposite side of the street and a good distance away from Tim's shop.

The door was unlocked as Tim had said it would be.

The four men walked inside and groped around in the dark.

Slocum walked back to the safe after telling the others to stay where they were and keep their eyes open.

He came back a few minutes later with a smile on his face.

"Tim left a can of glue right in front of that safe," he said. "So now you can bring in the dynamite, caps, and fuse, Del. José and Carlos can help you if you need it. Be careful with the sticks and don't drop the box of caps."

"I won't," Del said. "You boys come with me," he said to the two Mexicans. They followed him out of the store and José closed the door very quietly.

Slocum waited. He knew he was going to need light to work, but he didn't want anyone to see it from the street. He walked back to the safe and then back into the front part of

151

the store. As his eyes became accustomed to the darkness, he saw Tim's hurricane lamp and looked at the tables.

When the three men returned, carrying the explosives and other materials, he knew what he had to do to blow the safe.

Slocum slipped on his gloves and took the coil of fuse from Carlos.

"Carlos, bring that lamp into the room where the safe is. Del, you and José unload that stuff in there, too, then come back and get this table and bring it in. We'll stand it on end so that I can light the lamp and anybody coming by will have a hard time seeing the light while I work."

Del and José set down the caps and sticks of dynamite beside the wall next to the safe. Then they brought in the table and stood it on end.

Slocum struck a match and lit the lamp. He set it on the floor in front of the safe and shooed the others out of the room.

"Just wait until I come out," he said. "Keep your eyes on the street. Anybody shows up who looks like one of Scud's men, shoot him."

The three men walked into the front room and closed the door.

Slocum laid out the sticks of dynamite in an even row, with two inches of space between them. Then he took out his Bowie knife. He took one stick and lay it in front of him. He sliced the stick into two pieces with his knife and set the pieces aside. He did the same with all the sticks.

After that, he opened the box of caps and inserted them into the soft inside of the cut ends of dynamite sticks, burying the cap in the mixture of fine sawdust and nitroglycerine. He did this with each stick. Then he opened the can of glue and picked up the small brush that Tim had laid beside the can.

Slocum brushed one side of a half stick and glued it along the top edge of the safe's door. He did this with each half stick until the entire perimeter of the door was covered with dynamite.

He was sweating when he'd finished this task. He waited a minute or two then picked up the coil of fuse and stood up. He'd saved one complete stick of dynamite, which he cut in half, then pushed caps in both halves, cut two short lengths of fuse, and attached one to each half. He glued these half sticks at the top and bottom of the door so that they were near the sticks lined up around the edges.

He spliced the short fuse cords from the top and bottom sticks together, attached the remaining length of fuse, picked up the lamp, and walked into the front room, uncoiling the fuse as he went.

The other men all looked at him.

"Better clear out," he said as he blew out the lamp. "Leave the door wide open. I'm going to light this fuse and then run like hell. Del, you take my horse down to the end of the block. You and Carlos, fetch the wagon we spotted on the next block over. Hitch up those two horses Carlos and José are riding. Got that?"

The three men nodded.

"We'll load up the wagon and drive out to the adobe village and see who wants to ride with us."

"Where are we going?" José asked.

"Del here is going to show us where that Kiowa camp is. Maybe we'll get lucky and find Scud and his brother there."

"Godamighty, John, we goin' up against them redskins?"

"We sure are, Del. They stole four horses from me and I aim to get them back."

"If Scud is with them and his brother, too, there's going to be a hell of a fight."

"What are guns for?" Slocum asked. "Now clear out of here. I'll give you a few minutes to get down the street before I light this fuse."

The three men walked briskly across the street and

started untying their horses. Slocum watched them through the dark window until they were out of sight.

He took off his gloves and stuck them in his back pocket. Then he picked up the fuse, tucked it under his arm while he fished out a box of wooden matches. He struck the lucifer on the sandpaper side of the box, and a bright blue, red, and orange flame erupted. He touched the burning match to the end of the fuse, heard it hiss, and saw it spume smoke. He dropped the fuse, blew out the match, and ran through the open door. He ran to the end of the street, where Del was waiting with Ferro.

"Did you do it?" Del asked.

"Long fuse," Slocum said. "Might take a few minutes for the spark to hit the dynamite."

They waited. Slocum counted off the seconds, then lifted a finger to mark one minute, then two, three. Five minutes later, they heard a single explosion followed by a tremendous roar.

They both saw smoke billowing out of the gun shop.

"That will sure as hell wake up the town," Del said.

"Yeah, let's ride back and start getting at those guns."

The gun shop was filled with smoke and the smell of cordite. Del and Slocum tied their horses to the hitch rail two doors away and dashed into the smoke, removing their hats and fanning a path through the fumes.

The safe door gaped open. The metal on both sides of the seam was twisted and cracked. Inside, they saw shelves of pistols and stacks of rifles. They started carrying out the rifles first. They laid them outside and went back for pistols and ammunition. An empty wagon rumbled up the street.

On the seat were Carlos and José driving their horses.

Slocum hailed them as they drove up parallel to the shop.

"Start loading the wagon with those guns," Slocum said. "Keep your eyes peeled. We made a loud noise."

"We heard it," José said. He crossed himself and set the brake. Carlos jumped down from the seat first, then José climbed down, and the two men started loading the rifles, admiring some of them as they placed them flat on the wagon bed.

It took them a good fifteen minutes to get all the arms and ammunition. The table that had stood in front of the safe was blown to splinters. Smoke lingered in the corners and against the ceiling and bottoms of the walls like white cotton batting.

Slocum closed the door, looked both ways down the street, then unwrapped his reins and climbed into the saddle.

"Let's go," he said to José. "To your village."

"We are ready," José said, looking over at Carlos on the seat next to him.

"Keep your pistols and rifles handy. We're liable to run into some of Scud's men before we get to the diggings," Slocum said.

"We are ready," Carlos repeated.

José turned the wagon.

Slocum directed Del to bring up the rear while he rode in front.

The rifles clattered as they bounced up and down in the wagon bed. The pistols, most of them holstered, jostled with a sound like ocean waves in a squall.

The town stayed dark, and they saw no riders. When Slocum looked back, he saw a few lamps burning dimly from the houses on the back streets. He wondered if Tim was going to look over the damages and lock up his store. Slocum felt sorry about the worktable, but the gunsmith could easily build or buy another one.

They rode straight to the adobe village, where they all knew there were no guards. It was well after midnight when they got there. José drove the wagon to the center of the barrio and halted the horses. He spoke to Carlos, who ran to a friend's home while José climbed onto the wagon bed, picked up a rifle and a gun belt, and started yelling in his loudest voice.

"Come on, boys. We have guns. We are going to fight. Come and get your weapons."

As Slocum watched, sleepy-eyed men began to flow toward the wagon. Some were young, some older, but he counted a dozen who crowded around the wagon.

Carlos returned and started unhooking the team. He picked up their saddles and bridles from the wagon and started putting them on the two horses. One or two men came to help him while others grabbed rifles and searched for the correct ammunition.

When José was finished passing out the arms, he jumped down and walked over to Slocum, who sat his horse looking at the ragtag army assembled around the wagon.

"What do we do now?" José asked.

"You can stay here and wait for the day guards and take them down, or you can take over the sheriff's office and look for any of Scud's men."

"Do we shoot them or put them in jail?" José asked.

"Do you have a sheriff here you can trust? Do you have a judge who will try those men who kept you working here like slaves?'

"No," most of the men shouted.

"Then shoot any of Scud's men you find and tell everyone in town that they are free to leave. Tell them to pack up their goods and get the hell out of town."

"There are many who will leave," Carlos said.

"I think all of them will leave," José said.

Del rode up alongside Slocum.

"I know where the two day guards live," he said.

"Good," Slocum said. "If they're in town, we'll get them." He turned his attention back to José.

"March these men into town. Go to the livery stable. Do not harm the boy there, but take all the horses you can find and put them under saddle. I'll meet you there. I want at least ten men to ride with me and Del out to the Kiowa camp where Scud and his brother are."

"Carlos, start the men toward Polvo," José ordered.

Slocum said to José, "I'll meet you at the livery stable. About two hours from now, maybe sooner."

"We will be there," José said.

Slocum turned to Del.

"Let's see if we can find those two jaspers who work the day shift out here."

Del nodded.

"I know right where they live and we can get their horses, too, if we need them."

"The more horses we have, the better," Slocum said. "The soldier on horseback dominates the battlefield."

"I believe it," Del said.

Slocum waved to all the men as they started walking toward town. He heard the clicks of rifle mechanisms as they loaded their weapons. He heard José tell them to spread out and keep their eyes open.

"It looks like you got yourself an army, Slocum. Small, but they act like they're ready to fight."

"I just hope they're ready to kill," Slocum said.

No riders emerged from the town to challenge them as they cleared the outskirts. But the town was no longer asleep. Lamps burned in a number of windows and people were starting to mill around in the street. Many were streaming toward Tim Chandler's gun shop.

On the last street, Del turned his horse and pointed to the house where the two guards lived.

"That's it," he said. "And it looks like they're awake. See that lamp a-burnin' in the winder?"

"I see it," Slocum said.

That was not all he saw. There was a corral and lean-to shed out back. Shadows moved between the house and the shed. Two horses were already bridled and standing as the men threw on blankets, then lugged their saddles out to plunk on their horses' backs.

"Uh-oh," Del whispered. "I think they done spotted us."

Slocum sized up the distance between him and the men in the corral. Too dark and too risky for a shot and the coral poles blocked some of his view.

There was nothing to do but ride up on the men and brace them before they finished cinching up.

Del drew his pistol and cocked it.

"Wait," Slocum said. "Too far."

"I just want to be plumb ready," Del said in a low whisper.

Slocum did not draw his pistol. But he loosened his Winchester in its scabbard and kept Ferro at a steady walk toward the two men in the corral.

A cloud slid in front of the moon and the corral turned dark as pitch.

The two men and the horses might as well have been invisible. He could not see them. He looked up at the sky. The cloud was a large one and it was moving very slowly across the bright face of the moon.

The only sound he heard was the crunch of gravel under their horses' hooves.

And he knew that if he could hear it, so could the two men saddling up in the corral.

This was the most dangerous time, he knew. He and Del were high and visible on their hoses. The men in the corral were in a well of shadow.

It was, he thought, no time to flinch.

25

As Slocum and Del rode closer to the house and the corral, one of the men called out.

"Who's a-comin'? That you, Jube? Faron?"

"Maybe it's Oren," the other man said in a loud voice. "That you, Oren?"

"Sheriff?" the first man said, his voice turning into a liquid stream of uncertainty and perhaps fear.

The cloud slowly floated across the moon like a ghostly ship on a black ocean.

Slocum didn't know their names, so he could not answer even if he disguised his voice. He didn't want to know their names.

"It's me, Colter, Del," Del called out.

"What in hell you doin' here, Del? Did you hear that explosion 'bout an hour ago? Liked to shook us out of our bunks."

"I heard it," Del said. "Sounded like a boiler or some-thin'."

"Ain't no boilers in this backwater town. Me'n Ray are goin' to see what's up 'fore we go to work."

"What you want, Del?" Ray hollered as he pulled his single cinch tight.

Del did not answer right away. He looked over at Slocum, who was staring skyward at the moon.

"Nothin'," Del said.

"You off work?" came Ron Colter's brusque voice.

Slocum still could not see the men, but he knew they were going to lead their horses out of the enclosure and mount up. That would even up the odds too much.

He did not have to wait.

"Somethin' fishy goin' on here, Colter," Ray said. "Del, you better light down and walk over here where we can see you."

"Who's that with you?" Colter asked.

Slocum heard the creak of leather as a cinch tightened and the tongue slipped into its hole on the belt.

They were very close to the corral now and the cloud was drifting out into open sky.

Slocum and Del rode up to within a few feet of the corral.

"A—a friend," Del said when he saw the two men.

"You ain't got no friends, Del," Ray said. "You there," he said to Slocum, "who in hell are you?"

Slocum halted Ferro and turned him sideways to the corral. His hand sank to the butt of his pistol.

"The name's Slocum," he said in a deliberately loud voice.

"Slocum? Never heard of you," Colter said.

"Damn it, Ron, that's the name of the man with his picture on that dodger Oren gave us."

Colter cursed and grabbed for his pistol.

Ray went into a crouch and reached down for his pistol.

The cloud in front of the moon drifted into the blackness beyond, blotting out a few million stars, and light shone down into the corral.

Del fired off his pistol as both Ray and Ron drew theirs.

His shot struck a post, gouging out splinters of wood.

Slocum drew his pistol so fast that his hand was a blur of shadow. The click of the hammer was deafening in that moment of silence after the sound of Del's shot died away.

"Look out," Colter yelled.

Slocum squeezed the trigger, aiming for Ray, who was climbing the fence with his pistol drawn.

The bullet smashed into Ray's breastbone, splitting it as if struck by an axe. He flew backward off the rails and screamed on his way down.

Colter ducked behind a post and fired at Slocum. Del's horse shied away from the corral and stepped sideways as Slocum fired a slug into the post near Colter's head.

Colter stepped to one side to get a better shot after his first bullet whined off into space.

Slocum swung the barrel of his pistol to bear on the big man and he squeezed the trigger with a smooth flick of his finger.

The Colt in his hand belched fire and white smoke and the lead ball blew off half of Colter's jaw. He screamed in pain and pulled the trigger of his pistol without aiming the weapon. The bullet dug a furrow just to the left of Ferro. Slocum fired again as Colter's face spurted blood and broken teeth. The man choked and swung his pistol to close on Del.

Del swung his horse around and fired point-blank into Colter's chest, ripping through a lung and a portion of Colter's windpipe. He went down in a sprawling heap, his legs jerking like a chicken's with its head lopped off. Del fired another shot for good measure, and the bullet kicked up dust on the back of the fallen man's shirt. He twitched once more, let out a last groan, and then lay still, his vital organs shutting down.

"I got him, John," Del yelped. "I killed that sumbitch."

Slocum holstered his pistol.

"You sure did," he said and let out a long breath.

"Damn. I never thought I'd be the one who brought Colter down."

"Don't let it swell your head, Del. Pride goeth before a fall."

"Well, I got a right to be a little proud," Del said.

"Maybe a tad," Slocum said. "Let's get those horses and lead them to the livery stable. Two more mounts can't hurt."

"I'll open the gate," Del said as he swung out of the saddle, excited as a schoolboy on the first day of summer recess.

Slocum pulled out a cheroot and lit it while Del wrangled the horses out of the corral.

"Should I get their gun belts?" Del asked

"No, we don't need them. We've got their rifles." Slocum pulled out his pistol, ejected the empty hulls, and reloaded before he slipped the Colt back in its holster. He pulled on the cigar and drew smoke into his lungs. He let out the smoke slow and grabbed the reins of one of the horses.

"I hated that Colter," Del said as he mounted his horse. "He rode them Mexes like they were cattle, treated 'em like dogs."

"Then maybe there is such a thing as justice in this old world," Slocum said.

"You're damned right," Del said. He was still excited.

But as they rode back toward the stables, Slocum thought about justice. There was really none for the Mexicans, he knew. They were a cursed people even in the tolerant West. And they had a saying among themselves that he remembered very well. *"No hay justicia en el mundo,"* they said.

There is no justice in the world.

Even after you killed all the Colters in a cruel town like Polvo, there was no justice.

Not for the Mexicans and most everybody else who was dirt poor and ignorant of the ways of men and the snare of civilization.

Slocum knew it to be true.

He was an outlaw in name only, but it was enough to make him a hunted man wherever he roamed.

And, he knew, he would probably never return to Calhoun County, Georgia, where all his kin were buried.

26

Caleb Lindsey stood outside the stable, his hands high above his head, two Mexicans bracing him with rifles. His hair was mussed, his face contorted in fear.

Slocum rode up first and spoke to the two Mexicans.

"No molestas el gringito," he said.

The Mexicans laughed and withdrew their rifles.

"What did you say to them, Mr. Slocum?" asked Caleb as he slowly lowered his hands. "And what's so funny? They're stealin' all the horses and tack."

"Steady, Caleb," Slocum said. "I told them to leave the little gringo alone and they're not stealing those horses."

"I recognize them two you got there, too," Caleb said, pointing at the two horses with Carlos and José. Those belong to Colter and Ray. And what about them in the livery?"

"The spoils of war, Caleb. I sent these men here to appropriate the horses in the stable, and we didn't steal these two. Their owners have no further use of them."

Caleb looked puzzled.

"They just give 'em up?" he said.

"Sort of, Caleb. The owners of these horses are dead."

"Oh. Say, what's goin' on anyway?"

"Maybe something like a revolution," Slocum said. "You go on home, Caleb, and tell your folks that if they want to leave town, they can pack up their belongings and skedaddle. Nobody's going to bother them or stop them from leaving."

"How come?"

"Because Scud isn't going to be around much longer. Now get on home, Caleb."

"Yes, sir. Oh boy, will my folks be happy to get out of this godforsaken hell."

Slocum watched him run down the street and disappear in the darkness.

Men were leading saddled horses out of the stable. They all had strapped-on gun belts and there were rifles jutting from saddle scabbards.

"José," Slocum said, "give up those two horses and tell your men to warn the town that now's the time to pack up and leave. And pick ten more men who will ride with us to that Kiowa camp. We'll probably be in for some fighting."

"I will do this," José said. He dismounted as men came up and took the two horses he and Carlos had brought.

Del rode up alongside Slocum.

"I got a funny feelin' 'bout all this, John," he said.

"About the horses?"

"No, about goin' to that Injun camp. Callin' out Scud and Oren."

"If you don't want to fight, just say so. But I need you to show me the camp. After you've done that, you can come on back to town."

"Naw, I wouldn't just up and leave you. I just got a feelin' in my gut, that's all."

"That's called fear," Slocum said. "We all have it. I'm not looking forward to fighting a bunch of Indians and the Scudder boys."

"But you ain't scared," Del said.

"Like hell I'm not, Del. Like the general said, 'War is hell.' "

"General Sherman said that."

"Yeah, and old Cumpy knew what he was talking about."

José walked out of the livery and came up to Slocum.

"I could only get six men with good horses," he said. "I am sorry."

"That's enough. Tell them to mount up and let's go find Scud and that worthless brother of his."

A few minutes later, Slocum, Del, and eight men rode in pairs out of Polvo, following an easterly course until they came to the town sign. Then Del turned his horse south.

"How far is it from here?" Slocum asked.

"To the Injun camp? 'Bout five mile, I'd say."

"Just take it slow, Del, while I ride back and talk to my recruits. I want to hit them redskins just before dawn if we can."

"I'll walk my horse," Del said.

Slocum let him ride on as he turned Ferro and looked over the men behind Carlos and José. He spoke to each one as they passed.

"You ready to fight?" he asked each one.

Each one nodded.

"You picked some good men, José," Slocum said.

"I did not pick them," he said. "They all wanted to come."

"They look like good men."

"They are. They will fight. They hate Scud and they hate the brother, Oren," Carlos said.

Slocum rode ahead to join Del. He looked up at the sky. He didn't know what time it was, but he saw that the Big Dipper had moved and the moon was on a downward arc. They could cover the five miles in about an hour at this pace, and by then he hoped there would be enough daylight to count heads in the camp, but enough dark to catch the Kiowa and the Scudders by surprise.

It was a long and slow five miles.

There was no road and few tracks that Slocum could see. But he noticed that they were now heading in an easterly direction again. He hoped Del knew where he was going. The land began to rise and change slightly. Here and there, Slocum could see little hillocks and even a few gullies and washouts from flash floods. He knew they were heading toward Palo Duro Canyon, but he was sure that the Kiowa camp would not be down in the canyon, though perhaps on high ground.

He held his tongue because he could see that Del was intent on what he was dong.

After what seemed an interminable length of time, Del slowed his horse then reined it to a full stop.

"See that little ridge yonder?" he said.

He pointed to the southeast.

"Yeah," Slocum said. "Looks like water or an earthquake pushed up some land there."

"Well, just beyond that long rocky dune is where that Kiowa camp is, near as I recollect. They's a kind of a low-lying plateau just over that little ridge and they got teepees spread out on that flat place."

"They must be close to water, too," Slocum said.

"Yep. They's a spring-fed crick runnin' right past that little mesa and lots of trees. It's like one of them A-rab things."

"An oasis," Slocum said, a trace of a smile curling his lips.

"Yeah, one of them." Del rubbed his nose with a finger. "Damn, one of them trees is makin' my nose itch."

"Just don't sneeze," Slocum said.

He kept a close eye on the sky as they sat their horses. José rode up to talk to Slocum.

"We are close to the *Indios*, no?" he said.

"Very close. We will wait for the dawn a little while."

"We are ready when you say it is time," José said.

"Let's ride a little closer," Slocum said to Del. "I want to listen before we see the camp."

"Sure. We can creep some closer," Del said, and tapped his horse's flanks with his roweled spurs. They moved several yards until Del held up his hand to halt the men behind him and Slocum. Then he reined up his horse and Slocum did the same.

Slocum cocked his head to listen. He still could not see the mesa, but he saw the tops of trees, a couple of live oaks brimming the dark horizon. He cupped a hand to his right ear and sat very still.

"Hear anything?" Del whispered.

"Nope. Not yet. Too far away maybe."

"We get any closer, they could spot us," Del said.

"This is fine, Del. We'll watch that sky and those stars just above the eastern horizon."

Del nodded without saying anything.

It was quiet except for the faint rustle of the horses, the creak of the saddles. Slocum could hear his Del's breathing and the beating of his own heart. Nothing from the camp except a deep silence.

It seemed a long time before he noticed a slight paling in the eastern sky. The horizon went from black to slate, and the slate paled. Then the softest blue crept into the sky, wiping out the slate, and the first few stars began to wink out, one by one. The moon hovered above the land like a dying orb, its luster draining out of it gradually.

Slocum turned in the saddle and caught José's eye. He held up a hand to signal that he should stay and then tapped his spurs into Ferro's flank. The horse stepped forward. Del rode alongside.

The mesa came into view. Slocum saw small teepees breaking the skyline and more trees, scrub pine and junipers, bushes that were still dark lumps in deep shadow. He halted and stared at the spaces in between the Kiowa lodges.

There was no sign of life.

Not yet.

He kept looking as the pale blue of the sky crept higher and more stars became invisible.

Finally, one of the teepee flaps opened and there was a rustle of stiff leather. A half-naked Kiowa brave stooped over, stepped out. He stood up and stretched his arms as he stood up, staring at the eastern sky. Then he walked over to the edge of the mesa, lifted his loincloth, and peed.

Slocum turned in the saddle and beckoned to José and the others to join him. He held a finger to his lips to indicate that they should make no noise.

The small caravan moved toward him, shadowy figures on horseback, rifles standing straight up, butts to their pommels. The leather creaked, and the muffled sounds of the horses' hooves seemed deafening to Slocum.

When José drew near enough to hear him whisper, Slocum spoke to him.

"Fan out," he said. "Surround both ends of the camp with your men. We'll ride straight ahead."

José nodded that he understood. He spoke to the men in whispers and they began to spread out, half going toward one end of the mesa, the other half to the opposite end. Carlos led one group. José stayed on Slocum's left flank, his rifle at attention as if it were a soldier.

"*Bueno, estoy listo,*" he said as much to himself as to Slocum. "I am ready."

The Kiowa brave dropped the flap on his loincloth and started to walk back toward his teepee.

Slocum pulled his Winchester from its scabbard and levered a cartridge into the firing chamber. The action made a loud metallic sound.

The Kiowa stopped and stared straight at him.

Slocum put the rifle to his shoulder and took aim at the

lone brave. He figured the yardage at about one hundred yards. The rifle was sighted in at twenty-five yards, so he knew he could drop the man by aiming where he wanted the bullet to go.

He lined up the rear buckhorn with the front blade and settled the sights on the Kiowa's chest. Just as the man started to walk, or run, Slocum squeezed the trigger.

In the silence, the roar of the rifle was like a thunder crack. The rifle bucked against his shoulder and the Kiowa took one step before the bullet caught him square in the chest. The Indian toppled forward, his right arm outstretched. A hole appeared on his naked chest and blood squirted out like a dark rope. He hit the ground without crying out a warning.

But the sound of the explosion lingered in Slocum's ears for several seconds. Smoke wafted away like a thousand ruptured cobwebs. Slocum jacked another shell into the chamber.

The camp came alive.

Kiowa emerged from their teepees, carrying rifles or pistols, and Slocum could hear them talking to each other in their native tongue. Some of them used Spanish words. They all looked around for an enemy.

Rifle fire opened up on both ends of the small mesa. Del picked out a target and fired. An Indian went down. José, too, shot a Kiowa who was going into a knee squat to take aim with his rifle. The man threw up his arms. His rifle went flying and he toppled to one side, one leg twitching as blood gushed from his throat.

"Good shot," Slocum said.

He tracked another Kiowa brave who was running toward a live oak for cover. He led him perfectly, squeezed the trigger, and the Indian went down, face forward in a long skid, still gripping his rifle.

Slocum stopped looking for Kiowa targets. He scanned the camp looking for a white man.

José and Del kept firing and now there were Kiowa bullets flying their way, high and wild.

Horses in camp began to mill around their rope enclosure. They whinnied and whined in terror.

A couple of braves ran toward the rope corral.

It was then that Slocum saw a white man step into view. He carried a rifle and wore a gun belt. He was tall and bent over as he crept toward a scrub pine where a Kiowa brave was kneeling with his rifle at his shoulder.

Slocum recognized the man. The last time he had seen Oren Scudder, he was as naked as a jaybird. Now he was fully dressed and armed.

Slocum sucked in a shallow breath and brought his rifle to bear on the skulking figure.

Just as he was lining up his sights, Scudder wheeled and looked in Slocum's direction.

Scudder brought his rifle up and took aim.

Slocum let out his breath and dug his spurs into Ferro's flanks. He hunched over the saddle horn and charged toward Scudder at full gallop, much to the surprise of Del and José, who stopped shooting for fear of hitting him.

Slocum rammed his rifle back into its scabbard and drew his pistol.

In that moment, he felt like had when he had ridden with Quantrill back in Kansas. He hugged his horse's flank and cocked his pistol as he lay his head on Ferro's neck.

Scudder fired his rifle.

Slocum saw the stream of sparks and flame, the puff of smoke spewing from the barrel.

Time teetered on tiptoe as Scudder's bullet screamed through the air with a vicious high whine.

Rifle shots popped all around him.

Slocum knew, in that terrible instant, that he was on a battlefield.

And men were dying all around him, spilling their blood on dry, baked ground.

Just as they had in Kansas when Quantrill's cavalry was in full charge along the Missouri border.

And still, the bullet from Scudder's rifle was speeding toward him like an angry hornet.

27

Oren Scudder's bullet.

It sizzled past Slocum's ear close enough so that it raised the hairs on the back of his neck.

And then it caromed off a rock and whined into space, a scarred and deformed ball of lead.

Ahead, the slope of the mesa loomed. Slocum fired his pistol at Scudder before he reached that obstacle. Then Ferro was climbing, scrambling and scrabbling up the slope to reach the top of the plateau.

Slocum lost sight of Scudder for a few seconds as Ferro climbed to the top. Then he saw Scudder waddling around in a circle like some demented man looking for a lost watch somewhere on the ground.

As Slocum galloped toward him, Scudder straightened up. His rifle lay on the ground. He pawed for his pistol and was drawing when Slocum hammered back and fired a second shot.

There was a word on Scudder's lips. There was a snarl there, too. Then the bullet from Slocum's Colt struck him high on the left side of his chest and spun him around in a half circle. Slocum rode right up on him and fired another shot into his left side, smashing through his lung, nicking the tip of his heart, and blowing a fist-sized hole on the other side, ripping out lungs and flesh, smashing through veins and arteries like some demonic pellet fired from the bowels of hell.

Scudder belched blood from his mouth and crashed to the ground. He voided as his sphincter muscle relaxed and sent up a stench in a cloud of invisible vapor.

Then to his right, something caught his eye. Men were yelling, Kiowa yipping at the tops of their lungs. But a man was in the corral and he was climbing aboard a horse. He slashed one of the ropes with his knife and rode through.

He headed straight for Slocum.

Jesse Scudder bore a striking resemblance to his brother, Oren, just as Melissa had told him.

Carlos saw Scud and ran in front of his horse, blood in his eye.

To Slocum's horror, Scud fired his pistol at Carlos just as a Kiowa was about to smash Carlos with his tomahawk. Scud's bullet ripped into Carlos's temple and his head burst open like an exploding melon. Brains and blood flew back and struck the Kiowa full in the face. Slocum shot the Kiowa and then turned his pistol on Scud's horse. He could not get a clear shot at Scud.

Slocum fired and his bullet smacked into the horse's chest. The animal stumbled and his forelegs crumpled and collapsed. Scud bailed off the horse's bare back and hit the ground standing up.

The horse thrashed and kicked for several seconds as blood spurted from its shattered chest.

Scud regained his footing and swung his pistol to bear on Slocum, who reined up Ferro a half a dozen yards away.

"Slocum, you're a dead man," Scud spat.

Scud cocked his pistol and his arm started to rise.

"Not quite," Slocum said as he aimed his Colt at Scud.

Before Scud could get off a shot, Slocum squeezed the trigger. His pistol boomed loud and a streak of flame and smoke burst from the barrel.

Scud's finger touched his trigger, but the bullet from Slocum's gun caught him in the shoulder and knocked him off balance. Enough to spoil Scud's aim. He fired, but his bullet flew wide of its mark and whizzed over Slocum's head with a whoosh of air.

Slocum rode up on Scud and looked down at him. Blood dripped down left Scud's arm, and the man winced with pain.

Slocum stuck his pistol in Scud's face, within less than a foot. Scud stared at the snout of the Colt as he brought his own pistol up level to a line of sight leading directly to Slocum. He seemed to know that he was too slow and that death was staring him right in the face. His mouth contorted into a snarl. His eyes flashed with hatred.

Slocum squeezed the trigger as rifle fire erupted all around him.

Scud's mouth opened as Slocum's bullet creased his forehead, shattering bone and blowing his brains to a bloody mush. His pistol dropped from his hands. His eyes lost their glisten and turned dull as smoke-tarnished pennies. His legs turned to jelly and he fell in a heap.

"You should have been roped and dragged," Slocum said to the lifeless man, "then hanged for good measure."

Slocum knew that Scud could not hear him. The man was dead. But it gave him a small amount of satisfaction to say those words over his corpse.

The firing died down and Slocum glanced around him. Del had a peculiar look on his face. There were dead Kiowa all around Carlos's body and a couple of Mexicans were bleeding from wounds. Some were kicking the dead Kiowa with rifles pointed at their heads in case they showed any signs of life.

Slocum ejected the empty hulls from the cylinder of his

Colt and inserted fresh rounds. Then he holstered his pistol and looked around for José.

"You seen José?" he asked Del.

"Last I saw he was chasin' two Kiowa toward the canyon," Del said.

A moment later, they saw José riding toward them. Smoke still curled from the muzzle of his rifle barrel and he had a look of satisfaction on his face.

Slocum waved at him.

José waved a weary hand in reply.

Loose horses and Indian ponies were trotting around in circles. The smell of burnt powder lingered in the air. The dead began to give off their sickly sweet scents. The sun cleared the horizon and vanquished all the heavy shadows, turned the landscape into a rainbow of bright colors, its angry tongues lashing from a brilliant orange disk.

"Now what?" Del asked. "I don't see no live Kiowa and you killed Scud and Oren."

José rode up and halted his horse. He looked tired, but elated.

"Burn all these lodges," Slocum said to Del. "After you help me catch my four horses."

"You see 'em?" Del asked.

"Yeah, they're over at the creek, still wearing their halters."

"Should be easy to catch," Del said.

"I will help you," José said.

Then he spoke to his men, who were starting to head their way, on foot and on horseback. A couple were soaked with blood. Blood dripped from their fingers, but they were all ginning with the glow of victory on their faces.

"Burn down all these tents," José told the men gathering around him. "Then we go."

Slocum, Del, and José rode to the creek and started catching up the horses. They grabbed their halters and led them away from the creek. José and Del cut portions of ropes and affixed them to the halters.

"What do you do with these horses, John?" José asked.

"I'm taking them to Charlie Goodnight on the Palo Duro."

"Do you need help?" José asked.

"It's always good to have company on a long trail," Slocum said.

"I wouldn't mind makin' that ride with you either, John," Del said. "Maybe old Charlie Goodnight might have a job for me."

"He's a fine cattleman," Slocum said.

They watched as the Mexicans set fire to the Kiowa lodges. They put some of the dead Indians inside the teepees and gathered up the ponies to take back to town with them.

"Looks like we've got a bunch of fine horseflesh in our cadre," Slocum said as they rode away from the burning Indian village.

"Some of the poor of my people are no longer poor," José said. He was packing Carlos's body on the horse he was leading. "I wish Carlos could be here to see what we've done."

"He may be watchin'," Del said. He pointed a thumb skyward. "From up yonder."

As they rode into town, they could still see the smoke from the burning teepees, but of more interest were the number of loaded wagons leaving Polvo. People waved at them and they all bore smiles on their faces.

"This might become a ghost town," Slocum said.

"I hope it does," Del said. "Wait until the rest of them hear that Scud and Oren are dead. I wonder if they'll stay or go."

"Did those mines produce any real wealth?" Slocum asked.

Del shook his head. "I doubt it. No mother lode, no big nuggets, just a peck or two of dust."

"Maybe that's why Scud named the town Polvo," Slocum said. "Dust. Gold or dirt, it didn't seem to make much difference in the prosperity of Polvo."

"Yeah, it don't seem to matter none now," Del said.

As they rode toward the Excelsior Hotel, they saw people loading wagons in front of their stores. Others seemed to be strolling like sleepwalkers in a daze, asking questions, looking for people they knew.

"Maybe you ought to tell some of these people that Scud and his brother are dead, Del," Slocum said.

José turned in the saddle and looked behind him. The Mexicans with the ponies and horses were talking to the people in the street, telling them about how Slocum killed Scud and Oren. They spoke in both the Mexican and English tongues.

"The news will travel," José said. "This is a small town."

Slocum listened to the Mexicans and smiled. Some of them were already tearing down the wanted posters with his likeness. They wadded them up and threw them down in the street like so much trash.

He smiled when he saw people leaving the hotel with their valises and bags. Mr. Parsons stood outside like a man dumbstruck at all the activity.

Slocum waved to him, but Parsons let his head droop and did not wave back.

"Del, you and José take my horses to the livery. There's somebody I've got to see before we leave town."

"Where you goin'?" Del asked.

"To the Desert Rose. I might have one last drink before I ride out."

"And maybe you want to say good-bye to that purty gal you talked to last night."

"Maybe," Slocum said. "If she's still there."

He handed the rope to Del and rode off toward the saloon.

People on the street waved torn-down flyers at him and grinned with pleasure.

Slocum felt a little like a conquering hero, but he also felt a great sense of loss. Scud and his cohorts had built a town, but ruined many lives in the process. He would like nothing better than to set a torch to Polvo and leave it like the Kiowa village, in ashes.

But he had had his fill of destruction.

All he wanted now was to drink some good Kentucky bourbon and to see a pretty girl smile one last time.

28

As Slocum was tying Ferro to the hitch rail in front of the Desert Rose Saloon, he saw Tim Chandler heading toward him on a loaded wagon. Tim waved. Behind came Jorge Alessandro and his family, all wearing hats and waving to him.

The wagons pulled to a stop and tied up. Slocum walked through the batwings of the saloon.

The saloon was doing business. Jack Akers looked up at Slocum when he walked in, a wide grin on his face. Slocum walked over.

"I've got some Old Taylor for you, Slocum. On the house. And we're usin' them wanted dodgers for ass wipes."

"Thanks, Jack," Slocum said, pulling out a stool and pushing his hat onto the back of his head.

Akers got the bottle and a glass, set them down in front of Slocum. He inclined his head toward a table and pointed a thumb in that direction.

"The gals over there have been waitin' for you. Seems like the men guarding them got shot about an hour ago by some Mexes when those boys were headin' out of town."

Jack poured the drink into the shot glass.

Slocum turned to look at the girls sitting at the table like a bunch of women at a sewing circle.

He toasted them silently, then slid off the stool and walked over.

Melissa arose from her chair and kissed him on the cheek. Then he was accosted by Fanny, who hugged him and peppered his face and neck with kisses.

Slocum extricated himself and looked at the other women, who were gazing up at him with worshipping eyes.

"I'm Susan Lindale," one woman said. "We haven't met, but if you're John Slocum, you're my hero."

"I haven't met him either," Darla said, "but I liked him the first moment I set eyes on him."

Susan and Melissa sat back down.

"Well, you can't have him, Darla. Remember our pact?"

Darla drooped her head in a sheepish attitude.

"Pact?" Slocum said.

The women all laughed in unison.

"While we were waiting for you, John, we decided to stay on here in Polvo and help run the Desert Rose. We decided to call ourselves the 'Canyon Courtesans.'"

Melissa smirked when she said it, and the other women laughed like jovial conspirators.

"The Canyon Courtesans," Slocum said. "It has a nice ring to it. Who are you courtesaning with?"

"Why, we thought we'd start with you, John," Susan said. "Take turns."

Slocum blushed. He held both hands up in mock surrender.

"I'm headed out," he said.

"Oh, you can stay one more night, can't you, John?" Melissa cooed. "Just one little old night."

Slocum felt hot under the collar.

He looked at the women, smelled their heady perfume, and saw the desire in their dazzling eyes.

"I guess time will wait for one man," he said. "What's a day here or there?"

The women cheered and Jack walked over with the bottle and the glass.

He set them down in an empty spot on the table.

"You forgot this, John," he said. "You may need another swaller or two."

Slocum sat down and poured bourbon into the shot glass. He lifted it in a silent toast to the women at the table. They all applauded.

Slocum drank and the women cheered him with laughter and smiled at him.

"Who's first?" Darla asked.

Melissa gave her a withering look.

"Let John choose," Susan said.

"Yes, yes," they all shouted. "You choose, John."

John looked each one in the face. His gaze settled on Darla, the tallest of all the women.

Darla gave him an alluring smile.

"How about all four of you?" Slocum said. "Isn't that what courtesans are for?"

The women arose from their chairs and rushed to Slocum, smothering him with hugs and kisses.

Slocum floated on a cloud of pure pleasure, drenched in the scent of perfume and the musk of adoring women in season.

Watch for

SLOCUM AND THE DEVIL'S ROPE

401st novel in the exciting SLOCUM series
from Jove

Coming in July!

DON'T MISS A YEAR OF

Slocum Giant
by
Jake Logan

penguin.com/actionwesterns

M457AS0510

GIANT-SIZED ADVENTURE FROM
AVENGING ANGEL LONGARM.

BY TABOR EVANS

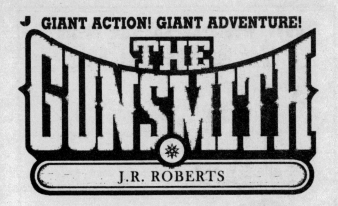

GIANT ACTION! GIANT ADVENTURE!

THE GUNSMITH

J.R. ROBERTS

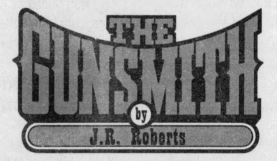